PRESCRIPTION FOR LOVE

~COLORADO DAWN~

BRIDES OF THE WEST
BOOK TEN

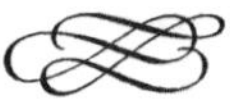

ERICA VETSCH

WILD HEART BOOKS

Cover design by: Wild Heart Books

ISBN: 978-1-963212-71-6

CHAPTER 1

New Orleans, Louisiana

June 1905

"Miss Morrison, until the mission board is satisfied that you have recovered fully from your illness, we will not send you back to Panama." Mr. Guillard tapped his papers into a neat pile and closed the file.

Her file.

Natalie pressed her lips together, trying not to let out in a rush all the things she wanted to say, knowing full well that Mr. Guillard was of a different generation, a man who had never been in favor of sending single women to the mission field and was always looking for either a reason for them to stay stateside or for young single male missionaries to marry them. She forced herself to speak moderately and respectfully.

"But I *am* very much better. I had almost recovered completely before I was called back to New Orleans." Natalie stacked her hands in her lap, consciously relaxing her muscles while maintaining her posture—though she could feel herself tiring. "I had thought to only spend a short while here before returning. Especially since there is a new team leaving in just two weeks. I planned to sail with them."

"While I can admire your zeal for your work, I cannot in good conscience allow you to return to the Panamanian jungles until you're more fit. You were laid quite low with fever for several weeks, and though you have been on the mend—if you'll pardon my saying so —you don't look particularly robust quite yet." He looked at her over the half-moon glasses perched on his bulbous nose. Mr. Guillard wasn't unkind, but he had a reputation for brooking no argument when he'd made up his mind. And evidently, he had the backing of the rest of the mission board on this at least.

Yet, how could she just accept his ruling? She needed to return to her work. Without it, who was she? Missions was her reason for being, what she was supposed to be doing, what her father would have expected of her. How could she be obedient to her calling if she couldn't even get to the people she was supposed to be serving?

"But, sir, what about my patients? The Ancon Hospital is short of nurses as it is. They need me." Her voice cracked.

"My dear, it is no shame to return home from the field when you've been ill. You were due for home leave soon anyway. The hospital will still be there when you are back to full strength. After all, as you said, we've a new team of four leaving for Panama City in two weeks aboard the *Caribbean Star*. Two doctors, an evangelist, and his wife who is also a nurse. They might all be new to the field, but they're good people."

Good people who knew nothing about what it was like to live and work in the tropical jungles of Central America. Natalie should be with them. She could help them transition to their new lives. After all, she had nearly five years of missionary service to her credit. To top it off, the evangelist's wife leaving with the group was a friend she had trained with, and Natalie had so looked forward to serving alongside Wanda in the hospital, teaching her the ropes of being a foreign missionary.

"For now"—Mr. Guillard opened another folder on his desk and scanned the top page—

"the director of the Marine Hospital is in search of a qualified nurse to assist one of their physicians in a new public health venture. While you are still not fully capable of returning to the rigors of hospital ward nursing, not even here in the States, much less in Panama"—he held up his hand to stay her protests—"your personal physician assures me that some light nursing is just what you need to keep your mind and hands busy while you regain your strength."

Natalie composed her expression, turning her head toward the office window that looked out on Rampart Street, where a motor car buzzed by in one direction and a dray pulled by a pair of shaggy draft horses clopping by in the other. Why did it feel as if everyone else was the motor car zooming past, while she was the slow old wagon plodding in the wrong direction?

Mr. Guillard cleared his throat, and she returned her attention to him with a guilty start.

"As I was saying, the city board of health is concerned about some of our...shall we say...less prosperous residents not receiving proper health care and education." He studied the pages before him. "There is a doctor at Marine Hospital who has proposed a new approach. Because these people, mostly immigrant and ethnic families...Italians, Irish, Jewish...they congregate together and are not very open to outsiders. Especially the Sicilian Italians." His brows hitched toward one another over his nose. "This doctor has a plan to...well, perhaps I should let him tell you when you arrive. Provisions have been made for you to move into the nurses' quarters at the hospital."

Which meant the mission board would not be paying for her room at the boardinghouse any longer.

A knock sounded on the door, and Mr. Guillard's secretary poked his head in. "I apologize sir, but your ten o'clock has arrived."

"Of course." He removed his glasses and polished them on his handkerchief. "Miss Morrison, Avery here will give you the paperwork you need. Present yourself to the Marine Hospital director, and he will take it from there."

"But, sir, if by some means I am able to satisfy the mission board that I am fit for travel in the next two weeks..." She left the question hanging as he rose and came to take her elbow, ushering her through the office door—not unkindly but definitely as if he was finished with the issue.

"I think that is highly unlikely. We will have another shipment of medical supplies going to Panama around Christmastime. Surely you can wait six months. Perhaps, in the meantime, you will find someone who will go with you." He raised his eyebrows and inclined his head toward his secretary. "Did I tell you Avery is preparing to go to the field by the end of the year? Perhaps the board will send him to Panama."

Mr. Guillard would never win a prize for subtlety. Avery Callan's eyes widened a touch, and he looked everywhere but at her face as a dull flush started up his neck.

Natalie took another calming breath. Mr. Guillard meant well, but he couldn't possibly know that Natalie had long ago been forced to close the door of her heart to anything romantic. She had taken up the stance of that greatest of missionaries, the Apostle Paul, eschewing romance in favor of the work of the Gospel —even though it had broken her heart and caused her to hurt the one person she had loved above all others.

Mr. Guillard bustled past, heading up the wide staircase to the conference room on the second floor of the old mansion that now served as the mission's headquarters. Avery cleared his throat, handed her an envelope, and hurried back into his cubbyhole of an office without a word.

Natalie found herself on the top step outside, looking up Rampart Street. All the city smells swirled around her—smoke, cabbage, dirt, even a faint whiff of the river a few blocks away. The June afternoon was warm, though she was accustomed to hot weather. And some of the smells were similar to her beloved Panama, that hot, vegetation-and-mud smell she knew so well.

The envelope in her hand drew her attention. Mr. Guillard had already had it prepared before she even came to the appointment, so it wouldn't have mattered what she said to him in their meeting. His mind had been fully made up.

She had two weeks. Or she had six months. Either she would make great strides in regaining her strength and convincing the mission board to allow her to return to Panama, or she would have to wait six months.

Six wasted months.

~

*H*e'd already wasted nearly six months, but such was the nature of pushing a new idea through government bureaucracy. Finally, he was finished with red tape and committee meetings.

Dr. Phineas Bartholomew Mackenzie swiped his black hair out of his eyes, reminding himself he was past due for a trip to the barber, and checked the inventory list one last time.

"This is it. They've approved everything I asked for. It's finally going to happen."

"That's astonishing." His friend and fellow doctor, Brian Trasker, leaned back in his chair and propped his feet up on Phin's desk. "How is it you get everything you want for that golden—excuse me—black chariot of yours, and I can't even get a brace of new bedpans for the surgical ward?" He laced his fingers over the front of his rumpled white coat and closed his eyes.

"Perhaps because I actually filled out the requisition forms and attended the meetings and pleaded my case, and finally practically kidnapped the hospital director and drove him through Little Palermo to show him how bad things were and where I thought we could help?" Phin grinned.

"Or, perhaps, it was because you were born with a silver spoon in your mouth, and the director didn't want to offend you or your parents who just happen to be friends of the president and the surgeon general, both of whom just happen to be his bosses?" Brian said it teasingly, not opening his eyes. He'd just come off a long overnight shift that had involved an emergency surgery and stitching up several stevedores who had gotten into a brawl sometime after three in the morning. His hilarious recounting of the drunks in the examining rooms had made Phin's sides hurt with laughing.

Phin sighed now. If Brian only knew. That silver spoon he'd supposedly been born with was a complete myth. He'd come into the world on a flatboat barge somewhere south of St. Louis, abandoned to the care of an uncle who was a petty thief, and eventually dropped into a St. Louis orphanage with many promises that the uncle would return to reclaim him.

Another in a long string of lies he'd been told.

Though the part about his parents—his adoptive parents—was true. They were well off, and they were friends of both President Roosevelt and the surgeon general. But that was neither here nor there. If Sam and Ellie's influence had come to bear on Phin's project, even obliquely, it hadn't been at Phin's behest.

Sam and Ellie.

Phin laid his pen on the blotter and picked up the silver-framed picture on the credenza behind him. His lips twitched as he took in the image of his thirteen-year-old self, stiff as if in full rigor, wearing a new suit and collar. He quickly looked past himself to the others in the photograph. His father, Sam, broad-shouldered, sandy-haired, blue eyed. His mother, Ellie, only six years older than himself that Christmas when she'd married Sam and took on two orphaned boys as her own.

Then there was his adopted brother, Tick. Michael,

Phin corrected himself. Nobody called him Tick anymore. It was a nickname Phin had given the small boy back at the orphanage because he stuck so close to Phin all the time.

He'd been a little gupper at the time, frail, with a heart condition that stunted his growth and kept him from thriving.

Though with care and medication, he'd overcome the odds and grown into adulthood. Now he was a pastor.

A pastor who was finally moving to New Orleans to begin a new church plant and ministry. Phin and his brother would be reunited once more.

"You look moony. Homesick for the mountains?"

Phin glanced up at Brian who had cracked one eye open.

"No. I haven't lived in the mountains since I was a kid. I told you the family sold out all their silver mines before the market crashed. We moved back to St. Louis when I was fifteen. It's not the mountains I miss. It's the people."

"I've never met anyone who was so close to his family as you are. You talk about them as if you were all best friends." Brian yawned. "Makes me jealous. I've never been that way with my family. We all live right here in New Orleans, and we barely see one another."

"My family is all I can count on." The only ones who have never left me on my own.

"What about me?" Brian dropped his boots to the

floor and stood, stretching and rubbing his stomach. "Are you saying you can't count on me?" He scrubbed his hands through his sandy hair and then smoothed it back.

Phin shook his head. "It's different. Family's just different. At least my family is."

"Well, let's go see this contraption of yours then I'm falling face-first into the closest bunk. And if a dock worker shows up wanting some needlework done, you're on your own. I sewed enough stitches to make a ball gown last night." He yawned again.

Phin slipped the inventory list into a desk drawer. "I need to stop by the dispensary and get a couple of things on the way."

When they finally arrived at the back courtyard of the Marine Hospital, both Phin and Brian had their arms full of glass bottles. Phin's pockets bulged with medicine packets too. "You know you could've gotten an orderly to carry this stuff out here. That's what orderlies are for." Brian shifted his load.

"They're busy, and we were coming out anyway. Isn't she a beauty?" Phin strode up to the ambulance, which gleamed black and shiny in the afternoon sunshine. The high wheels were dark red, and MOBILE DOCTOR'S OFFICE had been painted on the sides of the vehicle in bright gold lettering. The words had been repeated in smaller letters in Italian, Gaelic, and Hebrew. The sides had screened windows on the upper halves to let in air and light, and he'd had some nifty shelving built in to hold all the supplies he would need.

"You'll look like a gypsy. All you need are some bells and some pots and pans dangling from the roof and you can masquerade as a tinker." Brian set his armload of quart bottles on the ground beside one of the rear wheels.

"Very funny. I think she looks great." Phin ran his hand over the glossy paint. "This way, I can go right into the neighborhoods and treat people who would never come to a hospital or doctor's office."

"You're a brave man. I wouldn't want to head into Little Palermo alone."

"I won't be alone."

"Besides your driver, I mean." Brian helped Phin unload his supplies, careful not to break the containers of alcohol, camphor, and disinfectant.

"Actually, it will be more than just my driver going along, though I don't know if that means more or less protection." Phin grinned. "I've got a nurse."

"A nurse?" Brian's jaw dropped. "Are you serious? I can barely get a nurse to assist in surgery, and you just snap your fingers and the boss approves one to drive around town with you? Who is it?"

"I don't know. I just heard that I had been assigned one."

"You have some sort of Midas touch when it comes to persuading people." Brian shook his head. "I'm trying hard not to be jealous right now. I tell you what, turn your attention to the surgical department next, will you? I could use a new sterilizer, new lighting, and at least three new nurses, preferably with surgical training."

Phin laughed. "I'll see what I can do."

"I can't wait to meet the woman who will have to spend every day touring the slums with you. Think she'll be young? And pretty?" Brian waggled his eyebrows. "Will New Orleans's most eligible bachelor finally be snared?"

Phin sobered. "Not me. I'm immune from matrimony."

"I've never understood how someone so close with his family wouldn't want to start one of his own. It's not like the society mamas of New Orleans haven't pushed enough debutantes your direction." Stepping back as Phin swung open the rear door of the wagon, Brian waited for him to climb in before handing up the medicines.

Phin didn't reply. He'd been down the romantic road once before, and that was enough to last him a lifetime. There was no way he would trust his heart to another female again, not after having it handed back to him by the only woman he would ever love.

He hadn't been enough for her.

So she'd abandoned him.

"I doubt the new nurse will be young or pretty. More like a forty-year-old, built like a molasses barrel and smelling of cabbage and peppermints. Someone my great-aunt Tabitha would call 'a comfortable soul'." Phin slotted bottles into the racks built especially for them. "And I won't care a bit. As long as she knows how to treat patients, follow medical orders, and possibly speaks a bit of Italian, she'll be perfect."

"Really?"

A feminine voice.

Phin froze, his eyes locking with Brian's, who still filled the back door opening. Brian pulled a shocked, guilty face and slowly turned around.

"I can assure you that I do know how to treat patients, I can follow medical orders, and while I only know a smattering of Italian, I can speak a bit of French and am fluent in Spanish."

Brian sent him a 'you're-in-so-much-trouble-now' look and stepped aside. Phin braced himself, edged out of the wagon, and leapt to the ground. The minute his feet hit the pavement, his heart jolted into a gallop.

This was his new nurse?

<h1 style="text-align:center">CHAPTER 2</h1>

atalie's eyes met the doctor's, and her head spun as if she still had Yellow Fever.

Phin.

Dr. Phineas Bartholomew Mackenzie.

Her mouth went dry, and her thoughts whirled as she scrambled to organize them. Those beautiful dark eyes...so dark they glittered. Black hair still falling over his forehead. Thin...too thin, she'd always thought, with angular shoulders and long limbs.

Clean-shaven as always, he still gave off the impression that he was bursting with intelligence and energy, his mind always two or three steps ahead of everyone else. Dressed impeccably, knife-edge creases on his pants, snowy laboratory coat, neatly knotted tie, always the best-clothed man in any room. Even his watch-chain glittered in the sunlight, polished to a gleam.

He was the best-looking, smartest, quickest-minded man she had ever met.

Though he never thought of himself that way, as better than others or smarter than others.

Everything about him, remembered, dear, precious...and...forbidden.

Her mind jerked back to that night, on his family's yacht, in the Mississippi moonlight where he had proposed, getting down on one knee, offering her his heart, his love, and his future.

And she—who had been warring with herself for weeks that summer about what God wanted versus what she wanted—had been forced to refuse.

Something flashed for just a moment in his eyes just now. Was it pain, anger, or just surprise?

"Hello...Dr. Mackenzie. It's nice to see you again." She called him by his title out of a mixture of protocol and self-preservation. Holding out her hand, she waited to see what he would do.

His eyes flashed again, but his face gave away nothing of his feelings—he'd always been good at masking those, assuming a devil-may-care attitude and pretending that nobody could hurt him. Was that the truth in this case? After all, it was almost five years since she'd left. Perhaps for him, it had all faded into distant memory.

He grasped her hand for an instant, and his touch made her heart throb like a jungle drum. "Miss Morrison. What a surprise." He loosened his touch, and she resisted the urge to tuck her fingers into a fist and hold them behind her back.

She noted that he didn't say it was nice to see her.

The other man cleared his throat. "I take it you two know each other?"

"Brian," Phin's voice was as dry as mummy dust. "May I present Miss Morrison?" His black brows rose. "It is still *Miss*, isn't it?"

"Yes." Her chin went up.

"Of course it is. Miss Morrison, this is Dr. Trasker." Phin edged aside his long coat and put his hands into his pockets. "I take it you're the nurse assigned to the Neighborhood Health Project?"

She shook Dr. Trasker's hand, the good doctor holding her clasp longer than Phin had, his eyes appraising first her and then Phin, clearly curious but thankfully not asking what their connection had been.

"I am, though..." She fingered the cameo pin on her collar. "Only for six months at the longest. That's when I return to Panama." He might as well know this was a temporary situation at best. Perhaps she should ask the director for a different position...before Phin took it upon himself to refuse her the job.

"Six months, huh?" He rocked on his well-shined toes. "I'm surprised you can bear to be away that long."

An orderly stuck his head out the back door, saving her a reply. "Excuse me, Dr. Trasker. You're needed in the surgery."

With a frown, Dr. Trasker shook his head. "This had

better not be more dock workers." He gave a low wave to Phin and a nod to Natalie. "Nice to meet you Miss Morrison. I hope we'll have more time to talk in the future, and I wish you well with this new venture."

When the hospital door closed behind him, Natalie took a deep breath. "I'm sure the director can find another nurse for you."

He smoothed back his forelock. "Quitting so soon?"

She quelled a flinch. "Of course not. I assumed that our past...association...would lead you to choose another nurse. Not to mention, I will only be able to stay six months at the longest. This position isn't permanent for me. Another nurse makes better sense for you."

He considered her comments for a moment and then shrugged. "That's not necessary. We're both professionals, and anything that happened between us is long in the past. Water past the levee, for sure. You might as well be useful for the short time you're here." He looked her over, his gaze sharpening. "You look...different. Have you been unwell?"

His powers of observation as a physician were all too keen. "I am quite well, thank you." She straightened her shoulders and made an attempt to look bright. He didn't need to know what had brought her back stateside. "I'm ready to tackle a little light nursing before returning to the mission field."

"Light nursing?" The corner of his mouth quirked

up in a familiar way. "Didn't the director tell you what you would be doing?"

"He said I would be accompanying a doctor on house calls." Just about the lightest nursing there was.

For a moment, a small chuckle escaped Phin's lips, and she expected him to laugh, but he suppressed any lightheartedness. Disappointment wriggled through her chest. She had always loved his laugh, the way his eyes sparkled, the way his teeth flashed. That laugh had stalked her dreams at times, waking her up with such a sense of longing and loss that she'd sometimes cried herself back to sleep.

"I suppose that's true. Here." He stepped back. "Take a look inside and tell me what you think, and I'll explain."

She mounted the small iron steps into the wagon, ducking and taking a seat on the bench. Racks of medicines and shelves of instruments covered the end wall behind where the driver would sit, and a mattress covered a narrow bed along one side for transporting patients. Everything gleamed, fresh and new.

"It's a mobile doctor's office. There are more supplies under the bench too." Phin stood in the doorway. "Everything I might need, medical and surgical, though we'll only do surgery in the field if it's too dangerous to transport the patient back here to the hospital."

She ran her hand along the leather seat. No cloth here, easier to disinfect patent leather. "It looks wonderful, but I don't understand. Why don't the patients just come to you? Or have their local physician treat them?"

Phin pulled himself all the way up and into the wagon, taking a seat opposite her on the bed. "Most of the people we're going to see would never come to a hospital, and most don't have a physician at all. The part of town that used to be the French Quarter is almost entirely populated by Sicilian Italians with no money, very little English, and a big distrust of anyone in authority. Most of the men will be leaving the city to work on the plantations and farms in the outstate area, leaving behind their wives and children. The tenements are packed to the gills now, with most families only renting a single room. We're talking sometimes eight to ten people all living together in maybe a hundred or a hundred and twenty square feet of space. The poverty will shock you."

Natalie shook her head. "I doubt that. Panama is not a wealthy country by any means. The native Panamanians have similar fears of modern medicine and hospitals, though we're slowly making inroads. While the current building of the canal has brought some money into the country, for the most part, it remains as isolated and backward as ever. If anything, the influx of engineers, builders, and the military has made them distrust Americans even more." She clasped her hands in her lap. "We've discovered that if we start with the children, we can befriend and win the trust of the family. It's only then that we can share the gospel and expect to have it received. It's no good going into an area of extreme poverty and need and telling the people that God loves them and they need a Savior but do nothing to meet their physical needs at the same time."

He sat back and stared somewhere over her shoulder, and she realized she had climbed up on her hobby horse and ridden like she was chasing down the leader at the Crescent City Derby. And he clearly wanted to hear nothing about it.

"Tell me more about what you're hoping to accomplish."

His attention came back to her, and he smoothed his trouser legs, aligning the creases. "The first thing I would like to accomplish is to get medical help to where it is needed. There are sick and dying immigrants in Little Palermo, and I know I can help them, if they'll just let me. The second will be to educate these folks out of some of their suspicions. In Sicily, where most of them are from, there is a rumor—and I have no idea if it's true or not—that if you become ill, the authorities will hasten your demise by having a doctor or nurse poison you, thus relieving society of the burden of caring for you. If we do manage to get a Sicilian to the hospital, they refuse to take any water or food. Forget trying to get medicine into them." He shook his head. "And third, I want to educate these folks on the necessity of basic hygiene and cleanliness, and the dangers of open cisterns as breeding grounds for mosquitoes. With Dr. Walter Reed's findings, it's of paramount importance that we minimize the places that mosquitoes can flourish."

Phin's face was animated, his eyes alight, and he drew a poker chip from his lab coat pocket, walking the small circle of wood up and down the backs of his knuckles.

Natalie smiled. "You still have that?" She gestured to the chip, once red, but now without much paint left. "Still practicing?"

He glanced down as if he hadn't even been aware of what he was doing, and shrugged, slipping the chip back into his pocket. "You never know when you might need to pick a pocket. At least keeping my fingers nimble has paid off well during surgeries." Putting his hands on his knees, he levered himself up, crouching slightly inside the ambulance and heading toward the door.

When she followed him, he helped her down, but he didn't meet her eyes, and he let go of her elbow the instant her shoe touched the ground.

"Are you sure you don't mind? My working here the next six months?" Somehow, the moment she'd seen Phin, all thoughts of trying to convince the mission board she was strong enough to return in just two weeks had flown right out of her head.

"It's fine. I'd like you to familiarize yourself with the contents of the wagon and where everything is kept, and if I've missed anything you think we might need. I'd like to leave here each morning at eight." He studied her again. "Are you sure you're up to this? The days might be long, depending upon what we find."

Another orderly trotted down the back stairs. "Dr. Mackenzie, you have a visitor. I showed him to your office."

Phin's brows rose? "A colleague?"

The orderly frowned. "He said to tell you 'Tick' had arrived?" The young man shook his head. "I'm sorry, sir. I know that can't be right, but that's what it sounded like."

Phin was already on his way to the door, the tails on his lab coat billowing out behind him in his haste. "Thank you, Barker. I'll see you in the morning, Miss Morrison."

The screen door slammed behind him, and he was gone.

Natalie glanced at the orderly, who seemed as bemused as she felt. He nodded and hurried away.

She drew her first deep breath since she'd looked once more into Phin's dark eyes. Six months as his nurse. He had shown no emotion beyond mild surprise at seeing her. Perhaps they could make this work. They were professionals, after all, and adults. They had a common goal of helping people through medicine.

Natalie only hoped her heart would cooperate with her head. It had nearly wrecked her completely to leave Phin the first time. She didn't know if she would have the strength to do it again. She would have to guard her feelings closely and remember her promise to her father. She belonged on the mission field.

Nothing had changed in five years.

Phin bounded up the stairs to his third-floor office, trying to outrun the feelings that had come swamping back when he'd looked into Natalie's eyes.

It had been all he could do to appear unaffected.

He hurried down the hallway, sidestepping a nurse carrying a stack of clean linens and a janitor slowly mopping the linoleum tiles. Pushing open his office door, he said, "It's about time, Tick."

His adopted brother, Michael, rose from his chair to his full height, more than three inches taller than Phin. His shoulders were so broad, and yet so thin, Phin had the impression that Michael's black suit coat hung on a hanger instead of on his lean frame.

Though Phin held out his hand, Michael ignored it and enveloped him in a hug. "Hey, big brother. It's been far too long."

Phin returned the hug briefly. He slapped his brother on the shoulder. "It's good to see you again. I can't believe you're finally here."

Michael resumed his seat, folding his long frame into the chair. "Mother and Dad send their regards. They're hoping to visit New Orleans in the late summer or fall."

Rounding his desk, Phin took his seat, leaned back, and propped his feet up on the blotter. "Though I would love to see them, maybe they would prefer to wait until the fall when it isn't so beastly hot. You know how the heat bothers Mother."

Michael nodded. "I know, but you also know how she is about her cubs. She is worried that you're working too hard down here, and she's determined to come and check on you. In fact, you should know, she expects me to send her a full report as soon as possible, though she won't trust half of it until she can see for herself that you're not wasting away down here."

He closed his eyes for a moment, remembering his adoptive mother with fondness. She might be little, but when it came to her "cubs" she could go full-bore grizzly in their defense. He also knew much of her concern about how he was faring was a result of how badly he'd taken the breakup of his romance with Natalie five years ago. When he looked back on it now, he realized how hard he'd fallen. Weight loss, insomnia, throwing himself into work to avoid the pain, avoiding friends and family who had known how much he had been in love...picking up the pieces and feeling back to his old self...not that he would ever really feel like his old self...had taken time.

"What shall I tell her?" Michael asked, propping his ankle on the opposite knee.

Phin shrugged, shaking his head. "Like you said, nothing you tell her will be believed until she confirms it with her own eyes, so tell her I'm fine, hale and hearty, and that I am working on a new medical venture." He dropped his feet to the floor. "It's quitting time for the day, though. Let's go have some dinner and catch up."

"Great." Michael rose. "Let's swing by my new church, and then over dinner you can tell me about your new plans."

They took a streetcar, and when they alit, Phin slipped his watch off its chain and put it into his pocket. He took his wallet from his inside coat pocket and put it with his watch, covering both with his hand. "You might want to mind your valuables. This part of town is rife with pick-pockets," he cautioned Michael.

He laughed. "Anyone who stole my wallet would be mighty disappointed. I've got about four dollars on me at the moment."

Phin shook his head. Michael had little regard for money beyond what it could do to help someone else. Still, if he had four dollars in his wallet, he shouldn't be careless enough to let them be stolen.

They walked several blocks toward the waterfront before they reached the church. When they had climbed the cracked marble steps, Michael pushed open the carved wooden doors. The door stuck, and Phin bumped into Michael's back. "Sorry, Tick."

Inside, a musty, dusty smell hit Phin. The windows were boarded over, allowing only streaks of light to filter inside. Cobwebs hung from the pendant lights, and sheets covered the pulpit and communion table like cerements.

"What do you think?" Michael strode down the

aisle, stepping over leaf-litter and what appeared to be a mouse nest and turned to face Phin, arms spread wide.

Phin rubbed his forehead. "Are you sure about this? Your church in St. Louis was so successful. So big and nice."

Michael's expression grew sober. "Was it? Successful, I mean? There were a lot of people attending, I'll give you that, but the more people who came, the farther I felt from them. It became harder and harder to really connect with my parishioners, to really pastor them and for us to share accountability. I feared the church was becoming more of a social gathering than a place of worship. When I tried to voice my concerns to the elder board..." He sighed. "Let's just say, it didn't go over too well. Maybe I didn't explain it well. It just seemed like we were getting too far away from the mission of the church, which was to preach the gospel and disciple believers."

He mounted the three steps up to the dais and pulled the sheet off the pulpit. A cloud of dust enveloped him, and he waved it away. "Here, I feel needed. I feel like I can make a difference. There are so many here in New Orleans who need the gospel. They need to know someone cares about them, about their physical and spiritual needs. The groups we're targeting in particular are those who work the docks, and those who come in on the cargo ships. There are a core group of believers here in New Orleans who are prepared to volunteer, to pray, to give, and to help me and my team get this mission off the ground." A shaft of light fell across his face, and his eyes glowed with passion for his cause. "Tomorrow, the clean up on this abandoned church and the warehouse next door begins, and by the end of the month, we hope to have a soup kitchen and dormitory ready, and worship and prayer services happening. We've got a strategy in place to canvass the docks regularly, to meet the ships as they come in, and to get the word out to New Orleans residents so they can help. The more we get the word out, the more we can accomplish together."

Phin held up his hands, laughing. "Okay, okay. I've caught your vision. I'll help all I can."

Michael looked smug. "I knew you would. In fact, I'm counting on it. I have no connections here in New Orleans beyond the small group who called me to pastor this endeavor. You've lived here for years and must know plenty of people who can assist us. In fact, I'd like to visit some of the churches in the city to share our mission. Maybe you can put me in touch with someone who can help me set those meetings up?"

Over dinner they caught up on family doings. "Mother and Dad have been travelling a lot. They were in Boston, Philadelphia, and D.C. this past winter. They've been meeting with board members from state orphanages and private orphanages and with senators and congressmen about the plight of orphans in America." Michael leaned forward, knife and fork in his hands. "They've done so much for the orphanage where you and I grew up, using Aunt Tabitha's legacy." He smiled. "It wouldn't surprise me at all if they didn't find themselves in New Orleans with plans to open an orphanage here someday, since it seems you and I will be living here for a while."

"What about David and Karen and their kids?" Phin buttered a roll, remembering his aunt and uncle and their brood of six. "Their youngest is how old now?"

"Ten. And she's the image of her mother."

"And how is Celeste? It's hard to believe she's married and a mother in her own right now." Their cousin, once an orphan like themselves, had wed two years previously—the last time Phin had been home to St. Louis—and had produced a beautiful baby daughter the past winter.

"She misses you. They all do. You should plan a trip home soon. Our grandparents aren't getting any younger, and our cousins are growing up quickly."

"I know. I write often, and I do enjoy it when Mother and Dad come to New Orleans. As soon as I get this new venture off the ground, maybe I can make a trip home. Maybe even for Christmas." Christmas was the most important holiday for his family, a day to celebrate the Savior's birth, and also to celebrate the birth of their family. It was on Christmas Day nearly twenty years ago that Sam Mackenzie had proposed to Eldora Carter and decided to adopt Phin and Tick—Michael— in the bargain. And David and Karen had decided to adopt Celeste that day as well. After being unwanted, shunted from place to place, and enduring great hardship and peril, they had all become a family on Christmas Day.

"Tell me about this new thing you're working on with the hospital," Michael said.

So Phin did. With as much enthusiasm as Michael had shown for his new church and mission, Phin outlined the situation in Little Palermo, the needs of the immigrants there, and how he hoped to help them with his traveling doctor's office. "There's so much we can do in the way of public health education too. Most of this spring, the hospital director has been trying to educate the city council on the dangers of stagnate water as mosquito breeding grounds, and the need for a quarantine system for ships coming into New Orleans from Central America. There have been reports of Yellow Fever in those areas, and if it comes here, we're ill-equipped to deal with it."

Michael nodded. "Bureaucracy is hard to pierce sometimes."

"Hopefully we can teach people at a more grassroots level and bypass the bureaucracy."

"I don't know how you can make much progress all by yourself."

"I have to start somewhere. And I won't be all by myself." He broached the subject he'd been trying to ignore all evening. "And I would appreciate it if this didn't make it into any reports home to Mother and the family about it, at least not just yet..."

Michael put his cutlery down on the tablecloth and wiped his mouth with his napkin. "What is it?"

"The hospital has given me a nurse who will accompany me and assist me on my rounds."

"That's good. It sounds like more work already than one man can do."

"The thing is, the nurse I've been assigned is...Natalie." The word came out raspy, as if from long disuse...which was true. He hadn't said her first name in more than five years.

His brother sat back, brows raised. "I didn't know she was back in the States."

"I didn't either, until this afternoon. She's home for six months and then she'll return to Panama. In the meantime, she's been assigned to the hospital and to me."

"How do you feel about that?"

Phin knew he could never fool Michael, but he decided to try. "It's fine. All that happened a long time ago. We're not the same people we were then. And she's a good nurse."

"I see." Michael said the words slowly, and Phin knew he did see, more than Phin would like. He decided to change the subject.

"I'll pay for dinner." Phin set a few dollars on the table and waited.

"Nonsense. I'll pay my share at least." Michael patted his pocket, frowned, and searched his person. "Where's my wallet?"

With a grin, Phin removed Michael's battered leather wallet from his own pocket. "I still have the touch. I lifted this off you not half a minute after I warned you against pickpockets."

Michael took back his property with a sheepish grin. "Some things never change, do they?"

Phin hoped his brother didn't discover the money he'd placed in the wallet for a good while. Michael could be sticky about that sort of thing.

CHAPTER 3

The next morning, Natalie climbed into the hospital wagon and took her seat across from Phin. He held a sheaf of papers, and a frown built across his brow as he read them.

"Bad news?"

"Not good. The army reports out of Central America. They thought they had the Yellow Fever outbreak under control in Panama, but it's come back again. And there are reports of it spreading to Cuba and Belize. Things we knew. But there have been two suspicious deaths down near the waterfront that the director suspects are Yellow Fever." He tapped the pages together on his knee. "The city officials seem to think the ship quarantine and cleansing measures they have put into place will be enough, but scrubbing won't stop Yellow Fever. It's a mosquito-borne illness.Unless we control the mosquito population, if the Fever comes here, it will spread." He fisted his hand and tapped it gently against the edge of the bunk where he sat. "Why is it so hard to believe that mosquitoes transmit the sickness?"

Natalie said nothing, but her muscles clenched. Yellow Fever had come back to Panama? What of her friends there? What of the team that was going to leave in a few days' time?

"What can we do?"

He shook his head. "Be on the lookout for people with symptoms. Try to educate people about the dangers of unscreened windows, standing water, and not getting to a doctor if they feel ill. Beyond that, there isn't much we can do. One thing in our favor, it's been many years since there was an outbreak in New Orleans, but conversely,, it's been many years since there was an outbreak in New Orleans. People grow complacent. And they're slow to receive new ideas about disease. Dr. Walter Reed proved that the mosquito is the vector for Yellow Fever, but some persist in thinking that it's a miasma or that it only happens to new arrivals in the city who aren't used to the area. The hospital director wants us to be on the lookout for anything suspicious, and we're to gather information and report to him if we see anything that concerns us."

The wagon pulled to a stop, and they climbed down and stood in the sultry summer air amid squalor such as Natalie hadn't seen in weeks. So, this was Little Palermo in the old French Quarter of New Orleans.

Filthy water stood in pools in the gutters, and lines of laundry hung between the buildings. A famished-looking dog gnawed on a shard of bone, and from a crate beside a door, a pair of miserable chickens flapped and squawked.

The stench of mud, garbage, smoke, and unwashed humanity hung in the air, and Natalie pasted on her most serene expression, trying to ignore the assault to her senses. She'd learned early in her missionary career not to show any distaste or disdain for the living conditions of others. Compassion? Yes. Condescension? Never.

Phin jumped down from the front seat, lithe and handsome, his dark eyes sparkling with interest and adventure. After what had to be months of preparation and planning, he was putting into practice his dream to revolutionize medical care for immigrants. It was that zest for life and for helping people that had first drawn Natalie to him, and even now, she felt the familiar pull. But she couldn't. She wouldn't. She wasn't staying. Her life and work were a long way from New Orleans. Her calling was to the mission field.

Their driver, one Luca Todisco, sat with his shoulders hunched for a moment before wrapping the reins around the brake handle and easing to the ground. He was a giant of a man with fists like hams and a beard so thick and long that Natalie couldn't tell if he wore a necktie. He spoke English well but with such a thick

Italian accent, Natalie had to concentrate when listening to him.

"What do we do first? Do you have patients to see, or are we making a first foray?" Natalie smoothed the white apron she wore over a serviceable slate-blue dress. The hem was several inches above the ground, and she wore sturdy boots. A white kerchief covered her hair. Exactly the same attire she wore in the hospital in Panama. The outfit made her look both official and nonthreatening. At least that was her theory.

Phin reached into the wagon and took out his black medical bag. "We have no patients in advance. We're on a fact-finding mission today, assessing the situation. If we see someone in need of medical attention, we'll certainly try to help. But it would be unrealistic for us to be expected to be welcomed with open arms right away. We're going to have to build some trust. That's where Luca comes in, right Luca?"

"*Si, dottore.*" The big man grinned, his large, white teeth a glaring contrast to his swarthy face. "And I provide-a safety, yes?"

"Right." Phin squared his shoulders and walked to the front door of a three-story brick building. He eased the door open with a creak and a scrape, and Natalie followed him into an open courtyard. A woman with a black shawl over her head stirred a huge kettle in the center of the open space, black smoke pouring from beneath the pot. She looked up, eyes wide, dropped the wooden paddle, and backed away, her hands clasped at her throat. She felt behind her for a doorknob, and disappeared into a room with a slam.

"Dottore, perhaps-a you let-a me go first, yes?" Luca eased past Natalie, putting his big hands on her shoulders and gently moving her out of the way. When he reached the center of the courtyard, he tilted his head back and bellowed, *"Attenzione! Un dottore è venuto a visitare! Vieni fuori!"*

No doors opened, and several eased closed, though Natalie saw no one. No, wait. A pair of dark eyes peeped around a corner...small, bright eyes and a sweet little face. She smiled and wiggled her fingers at the child, a girl of about three, maybe? The youngster wore a smudged white smock-dress and no shoes and was in need of a comb or brush, but she was beautiful.

Natalie nudged Phin and inclined her head toward the child.

Luca scratched his head, turned and spoke toward the balconies surrounding the courtyard. *"Qualcuno qui è malato?"*

"What is he saying?" Natalie asked.

Luca answered. "I said that a doctor had come-a to visit and for the people to come out, and I asked if anyone was-a sick."

Phin inclined his head, watching the little girl, who had stuck one finger into the corner of her mouth and fisted her other hand into her dress, twisting it up to reveal her knees. "Maybe you should ask if anyone wants candy?"

"Hmph. You might-a be-a trampled," Luca said. "*Qualcuno vuole qualche caramella?*"

Natalie put her hand over her mouth to stifle the giggles. Children tumbled out of everywhere, behind boxes, through windows, down the stairs, through doorways.

Luca motioned them to come close, a torrent of Italian words flowing from him, accompanied by wide smiles.

Phin eyed them with a grin, and Natalie's heart lurched at his handsome features. He reached into his bag and pulled out a peppermint ball. With several quick moves of his hands, he made it disappear and reappear, to the gasps and giggles of his crowd. How often had he entertained children in the hospital with his slight-of-hand tricks? How often had he entertained her?

"Tell them they can each have a piece of candy if their mamas say it is all right," Phin said. His gaze moved from child to child. There must've been about twenty of them altogether. Natalie assessed them as well, looking for signs of any medical need.

Though quite a few would benefit from a bath, and there were the usual cuts and scrapes that went along with being a child, she could see no one in obvious distress.

Mothers were called, young and old, timidly venturing into the courtyard, encouraged by Luca. Phin greeted them, showed them his medical bag, and through Luca, spoke about the mobile doctor's unit, inquiring as to any illnesses in the building, any injuries.

While the women listened politely, Natalie knew they were skeptical. They offered no information, instead behaving as if Phin was a policeman or health inspector, someone to be deferred to but not invited in. They were facing an uphill battle here.

A commotion sounded near the doorway to the street, and a pair of children broke from the pack to run toward the man standing there.

"*Papà! Papà!*" The children threw themselves into the lean man's arms as he squatted to receive them. His duffelbag fell to the floor as he embraced them. Behind him, another man leaned against the doorframe.

Phin handed the sack of candy to Luca. "Here, make sure each child gets one." He picked up his bag and went to the doorway, and Natalie followed. Skirting the happy family reunion, Phin came to a stop beside the other man.

"Sir, I am a doctor. How are you feeling?"

Even across the courtyard, Phin has spied something about the man that caught his attention. Up close, Natalie noted the man's flushed skin and the bright glitter to his eyes that often denoted fever.

The man scowled and straightened. "Go away. I am-a not sick. I am-a tired." He hitched his seabag over his shoulder with a wince and brushed past. As he crossed a shaft of sunlight, Natalie stepped back. As she looked into the man's eyes, her senses went on alert.

She stepped close to whisper to Phin. "That man is jaundiced, feverish, and probably achy." She had reason to remember all those symptoms, since they were the early signs of the illness that had laid her low for so many weeks.

Of course, they could also be the early signs of other illnesses, and it wasn't reasonable to feel a rush of anxiety, but uneasiness fluttered across her skin.

Phin nodded, motioned for her to follow and went after the man, mounting the stairs to the second floor. The man ducked into the first doorway and closed the door. Phin knocked.

No answer.

He knocked again. The door opened a crack, and a woman's lined face peered out. "No. Go away." She closed the door with a bang.

"Ma'am, please. I am a doctor. Dottore. *Per favore.*"

The door remained stubbornly closed.

Phin's hands fisted, and he shook his head. "Stubborn man."

"What are we going to do?" Natalie asked.

"Let's start with the man downstairs. Get some information. Fever and ache are symptoms of lots of things, and I didn't see the man's eyes in the gloom of the entryway. You're sure they were yellowed?"

Her chin came up. "I believe I have enough medical and tropical nursing experience to recognize jaundice when I see it." Not to mention having both cared for and been a Yellow Fever victim.

"Of course you do. But everything must be verified." He was on his way down the stairs again. "Luca, I need you to translate."

Luca gave out the last piece of candy and motioned for the sailor with the two children to come to them.

"Ask him what ship he works on and where it came from and if anyone on the boat has been ill."

Luca spoke rapidly, gesturing with every phrase. The man's arms tightened around his children, and a wary look invaded his dark eyes as he glanced from Phin to Luca and back again. Luca grew stern as the man refused to answer his questions, repeatedly shaking his head and hugging his children.

Finally, Luca pointed to Phin and made some statement that sounded threatening to Natalie's ears. The sailor shot them a fearful glance and began to speak.

"He says-a he works on a boat that-a come from-a Belize. The boat-a carry bananas, and the *captiano*, he no wanna wait for the quarantine, so he slip past into the bayou at night. This man, he say that-a two of the crew were sick, but they are feeling-a better now."

Natalie crossed her arms, gripping her elbows. Phin nodded. "Ask him about their symptoms."

"What is 'symptoms'?" Luca's brow furrowed.

"Ask him how they felt. Did they hurt? Did they have a fever?"

Understanding dawned. "Symptoms, yes."

Again the rapid-fire speech back and forth.

Finally the sailor shrugged.

"He says-a he does not-a know. Just-a sick."

"Thank him for us. *Grazie*." Phin took Natalie's elbow. "We need to leave. We need to find that ship and the sailors who crewed it."

Phin climbed into the back of the wagon with Natalie as Luca took his seat. Opening the communication window at the front, he told Luca, "Let's get down to the docks and see if we can get a line on where they might unload a shipment of bananas without using the stevedores at the waterfront."

The wagon lurched, and Natalie grabbed the edge of her seat. "It could be something else besides Yellow Fever. We didn't ask if the man drank a lot of alcohol, which can cause jaundice. Or if he had any other symptoms. And the two suspicious deaths that were reported haven't been confirmed yet." Even as she said the words, she was totting up what they did know. Yellow Fever wasn't often mistaken for something else. There were confirmed reports in Central America. It was summer, Yellow Fever season. A sick man had come from Belize and bypassed the riverfront quarantine procedures. She was sure he was jaundiced. And the way he had winced when he shouldered his rucksack meant he was in some pain, possibly joint pain. And his eyes had been fever-bright.

Then there was the fact that the man they had questioned had said the men had felt bad on the journey but were on the mend now.

That sounded like Yellow Fever.

A few days of being really ill, followed by a few where the patient appeared to recover, only to become seriously ill once more. But maybe they were just reacting to the hospital bulletin Phin had received that morning. Perhaps it wasn't anything but a bit of a cold or hepatitis or too much alcohol.

Gripping her elbows again, she suppressed a shiver.

It was too soon to panic.

~

*P*hin took out his notebook and tried to jot notes as the wagon rocked and clattered on its way to the wharf. He had learned long ago that he needed to write things down to get clarity and be able to remember details later for writing up reports.

Hopefully, they were on a hiding to nowhere, and the men would simply have fallen ill to an ordinary malady. Perhaps the man they saw did have cirrhosis of the liver or hepatitis. He would go to the harbor, see if he could track down someone from the ship, and be reassured.

Natalie held onto the bench as the wagon jolted over the railroad tracks and headed down to the water's edge. She looked so prim and efficient in her nurse's garb, her glossy hair covered with that white kerchief.

The observations she had made about the sailor had been dead-on. She was a good nurse. He remembered the first time he saw her, a nursing student with wide eyes and an eager, wholesome quality. Even then, she'd had an instictive ability to soothe a worried patient and to hone in on symptoms.

And she had been able to make him laugh. She was sweet and idealistic, passionate, and she had a positive outlook that had complemented his more cynical side. He had been a perfect fit for him.

Until she wasn't.

Bitter regret clamped onto his chest. He couldn't allow himself any hope that anything would end differently than it had before. He had misread her completely once, thinking that she loved him enough to stay. He wouldn't make that same mistake.

Tracking down the doctor aboard the banana boat proved frustrating. Luca used his considerable contacts and not a little bribe money. When they finally found the ship's medical officer, he was three beers into his shore leave. And he wasn't really a doctor, just a sort of corpsman.

There was no need for a translator, as the man was an American.

"A couple of the men came down with a bit of a bug. A bit of a fever, a few aches. Nothing to be concerned about. They stayed in their bunks for a few days. Then they both said they felt better." He made small circles with his glass on the tabletop in the riverfront hotel that catered to arriving seamen. "And I don't know where the captain is, and I wouldn't rat him out anyway. So he bypassed those snoops down at the docks. They forever hold a man up so he can't unload and get paid. And they don't do no good, nohow. Poking and prodding everywhere, gassing the place with poison."

Phin had insisted Natalie remain outside with Luca and the wagon, so he took notes himself. "What about jaundice?"

The man squinted. "What?"

"The men who were sick, did their skin or eyes look yellow to you? Did they have any tenderness to their liver?" Phin pointed to his upper right abdomen.

Shrugging, the man drained his glass. "They never said so. Look, the captain calls me the medical officer, but I ain't. Most of the time, I work in the kitchen. I can sew up cuts and wrap up sprains and the like if I have to. I don't know one sickness from another." He shrugged again, raising his glass and catching the eye of the bartender.

Phin asked a few more questions about the number of crewmembers and where the ship had been, but the sailor either didn't know much, or was pretending no to know.

Emerging into the sunshine, Phin tapped his notebook against his leg. He needed to find that second sailor and see if he would submit to an examination. And he needed to check out the other crew members. If his suspicions were confirmed, he would need to inform the director at the hospital, the city health officials, and if necessary, national health officials.

"How do you find a crew full of sailors that the harbor master doesn't know exists in a city equipped to hide them?"

"You should be careful talking to yourself out on the street. People might think you're touched in the head."

Phin whirled and grinned. "Hey, Tick."

At the nickname, his brother slanted him an aggrieved glance. "No one will take me seriously as a minister if you insist on calling me Tick."

"Sorry. Old habits. What are you doing here?"

"Working. I've come to canvass the area for a few likely souls to fill our mission and first church service. And to put up these bills." Michael lifted a sheaf of posters announcing the opening of the Sailor's Mission. "There's a bunch of volunteers busy cleaning out the buildings, and you wouldn't believe the aromas already spilling from the old kitchen. The Mission hired a woman named Centralia, and she's cooking gumbo that's making me hungry just thinking of it. Once word gets out about her cooking, we'll have more sailors and seamen than we know what to do with. And she's doing it on a pretty meager budget too." Michael scratched his head. "I don't know how, but I'm just going to thank God for His blessings."

"That's great." Phin scanned the river, dotted with ships from all over the world. A sting touched his hand, and he slapped a mosquito.

Michael swatted as one buzzed by his face. "I have a reason to be here, but what's yours? I thought you would be out with your mobile office seeing patients."

Phin motioned for Michael to walk with him. "I am. Sort of. I'm trying to track down a ship that bypassed quarantine measures." He pointed to a steamship drawn up to a dock along the riverfront. A quarantine flag hung from the bow, and a pair of men were shooting a stream of hot water at the deck. "There's a report that some of them are sick."

Michael tugged on his bottom lip. "You know that cook I mentioned? Centralia? She gave me a tip on where to find some men who were new to the city and might need the sort of help we provide at the Sailor's Mission. A fellow brought her a crate of bananas this morning, offered it to her for cheap. Said it was off a ship that hadn't been forced to pay the harbor fees. He told her he was staying at a boardinghouse on Dauphine, and if she wanted more produce, to let him know. I swung by the boardinghouse this morning and invited them to the Mission."

Phin halted. "That sounds promising. Can you take me to them?"

"Sure. It's only a few blocks from here."

Phin resumed walking. The medical wagon stood just ahead, with Natalie and Luca beside it in the shade.

Michael caught sight of them and strode forward, forging ahead of Phin.

"Natalie, how great to see you again." He didn't wait

for permission, enveloping her in a big hug. "It's been far too long."

A stab of jealousy hit Phin, and he stuck his notebook into his coat and jammed his hands into his pants' pockets. Michael had always been affectionate, but seeing him hugging Natalie made Phin's own arms feel empty.

"Michael, or should I say Pastor Mackenzie? I had no idea you were in New Orleans." Natalie emerged from his embrace and righted her kerchief. "What a pleasant surprise." The smile she beamed at him would shame the sun, and again Phin fought down his feelings. Michael and Natalie had only met a couple of times to his recollection, but there had been an instant friendly bond between the woman he had loved and his brother.

"Michael, can you take us to the boardinghouse? I'd like to check them over as soon as possible." Phin pulled out his watch. This day was turning out nothing like he'd planned.

Natalie came to his side. "What did the doctor say?"

"Nothing useful. He's basically a glorified cook. Let's get moving." He held her elbow as he helped her into the back of the wagon. "We can talk on the way. Michael, this is Luca."

"Nice to meet you, Luca. You want to head to Dauphine between St. Peter and Toulouse." Michael followed Natalie into the wagon, and Phin jumped aboard, closing the door.

The only place to sit was next to Natalie. Michael had commandeered the pallet on the bench. Phin's shoulder bumped Natalie's as the wagon started, and he quickly righted himself.

But space was tight in the conveyance, and his leg brushed hers and their elbows touched. Awareness at each point of contact shot through him, ending at his heart, increasing its pace and making his breathing unsteady. He forced himself to concentrate on the task at hand.

"So, what is this about?" Michael asked, his expression open and curious.

"Just a feeling, but I want to look into it. There were some sailors who were ill, and the symptoms might be nothing, but they might be very troubling We received notice this morning that tropical fever outbreaks had occured where this ship supposedly came from, and there were a couple of suspicious deaths reported this morning in the city that are awaiting autopsy to confirm cause of death."

"Tropical fever? Like malaria?"

Phin shook his head. "Worse. This might be Yellow Fever."

The look on Michael's face confirmed Phin's feelings. Yellow Fever was the most feared epidemic in America. It came suddenly, struck in what appeared to be a random manner, and killed ruthlessly. The worst outbreaks in U.S. history had killed thousands. They now had a better understanding of how the sickness spread, but until they could convince citizens and leaders alike, the danger of widespread infection would persist.

When they reached the boardinghouse, Michael insisted on going inside with them. "I've met the men, down at the docks. I can introduce you."

Phin shook his head. "This isn't a social visit."

"Nevertheless, it might help to have at least a marginally familiar face."

Natalie followed along. "What if we find men who are ill?"

"Then we'll transport them to the hospital as quickly as possible."

"What if they won't go?"

She voiced Phin's fears. If the men were Italian immigrants, they would be resistant to going to the hospital. They would probably resist letting him examine them at all.

"Michael, now might be a good time for you to start praying." Phin opened the boardinghouse door.

"Start? I've been praying all the way from the riverfront."

CHAPTER 4

Natalie knew it the moment she saw the man, listless, yellow, and holding his abdomen, that they were in trouble. Her eyes met Phin's across the sickbed, and he nodded.

"Luca, tell him he must go to the hospital." Phin bent and examined the man's eyes and palpated his abdomen, which elicited a groan.

"Signore, devi andare in ospedale."

"No." Fear ringed the man's jaundiced eyes. He rolled to his side, moaning. A trickle of blood came from his nose, and Natalie reached for the towel on the washstand. The man flinched and reared back, putting his hands up before his face to ward her off.

Natalie looked at Phin. How were they going to treat this man if he shied away from every contact?

"It's the same old fears and superstitions from Sicily." Phin scowled at the ceiling. "Luca, tell him we mean him no harm. Tell him we're here to help him."

Luca spoke again, rapidly, urgently.

Natalie knelt beside the patient, putting her hand on his forehead, following his movement when he tried to shrug her away. His skin was paper dry and hot, and his eyes bloodshot. "Shhh." Gently, she used the towel to wipe the blood from his upper lip. "Lord, please help me know how to help this man," she whispered.

The patient's eyes never left her face, but his shoulders relaxed a bit. *"Tu pregi?"* he whispered?

She raised her eyes to Luca, who said, "He asks if you praying?"

Nodding, she clasped the patient's hand. He gripped her fingers, eyes locking with hers. She bowed her head and whispered, asking God to help them help this man, to take away his fear, to give them wisdom. As she did, the man relaxed, his grasp becoming less frantic, his breathing steadying.

"Stay with him while we talk in the hall." Phin touched her shoulder, the way he had countless times when he'd left her with a patient. He and Luca and Michael went into the hall, closing the door behind them, and she loosened her fingers to check the patient's pulse.

While most fevers caused a patient's heart rate to increase, Yellow Fever slowed the pulse down. This man's pulse was very slow.

She had read the medical reports of Dr. Reed and Dr. Finlay, heard of the death of Dr. Lazear in the brave battle to identify the source and vector of Yellow Fever. She'd sat through many educational seminars taught by military and visiting doctors to the Panamanian jungle. She knew firsthand the dangers, and she assessed them in this case.

The windows were unscreened and wide open. On the street below, the gutters had stagnated water pooling in the cracks. Every house had an open cistern for collecting rainwater, since there were no freshwater wells in this part of the city. Mosquito breeding grounds abounded, and there was nothing to keep them from biting this Yellow Fever victim and carrying the poison to the next person they attacked.

She took the man's hand between her own, bowed her head, and prayed. For him, for his family, wherever they were, and for protection for the people of New Orleans.

Phin returned alone and began packing a few of the man's belongings into his sea bag. "Michael and Luca are canvassing the building to see if they can get more information about this man. Whether he has family in the city and such. And to find more of his shipmates. For now, let's do a thorough examination, take some notes, and see about transporting him to the hospital."

Natalie wet a cloth and bathed the man's face and chest. He had his eyes closed, and he lay still, as if moving hurt too much to contemplate.

Michael returned first. "That man, Luca...when you

don't need his services anymore, I could sure use him at the Mission. He's talking to the first officer of the banana boat now."

"What did he find out?"

"There were eighteen men aboard the ship, the *Mendoza*. Only two were sick when they reached New Orleans, but since then, this man fell ill. His name is Mario Favaro."

At the sound of his name, the patient opened his eyes a slit and nodded. "*Si, signor*. Mario," he whispered.

Phin concluded his examination, pulling the sheet up to the patient's armpits. Natalie finished writing down her notes in Phin's notebook.

"And does he have family?" Phin asked.

"From what Luca gathered, the man left Sicily rather rapidly a year ago when he found himself on the wrong side of the authorities there. He came to this country alone, found work aboard the *Mendoza*, and has been with the ship ever since."

"We need to persuade him to go to the hospital. He's very ill, and with no one to care for him here…" Phin folded his stethoscope and tucked it into his bag. "Natalie, read back his information please."

Again a sense of familiarity swept over her. Phin always asked for a summation of an examination before he was finished. "Pulse 52, respiration 12. Temperature 102. Patient exhibits jaundice, back pain, liver tenderness. No vomiting as yet, but bleeding from nose. Signs of dehydration. Symptoms point to Bronze John." She used one of the common names for Yellow Fever, hoping that the patient wouldn't recognize it and panic.

Phin listened as he shook the mercury back down in the thermometer and handed it to Natalie, who wiped it with alcohol before returning it to the case inside his medical bag.

It took some time and much pursuasion and assurances both from Michael and Natalie via Luca's translating, but Mario finally assented to a trip to the hospital. Luca eschewed assistance, gathering the sailor up in his arms and carrying him out into the street as if he were a child.

As they rattled over the cobbles toward the hospital, Phin outline his plan.

"We'll have to isolate him. Mosquito netting around his bed, screens on the windows, and mosquito bars hanging everywhere."

Natalie jotted his notes, though she knew the treatment by heart.

"We'll start him on quinine and cool cloths to reduce his fever, and encourage him to drink. Keep the ward quiet and dark."

He was businesslike and professional, but as he spoke, he smoothed back Mario's hair and folded a towel to place over the man's eyes to block out the light. Yellow Fever caused atrocious headaches, and the darkness would soothe the man. He patted the man's shoulder. Natalie was warmed by his tenderness. Most people saw Phin as a sharp mind, quick of thought, quick of action, but she knew the softer side of him, the part that truly cared about his patients and their comfort and well-being.

Michael had joined Luca up front, and he stood by in the hosptial courtyard when orderlies came out of the building with a litter to carry the man inside.

Phin placed his hand on Natalie's arm when she went to follow them. "This may be the first of many cases, you know. Or it could be as simple as a couple of men, and no one else will get sick. I don't want to be alarmist, but I have to notify people and I have to return to the tenement where that sick man from this morning wouldn't let us in. Can you take care of things here? Hopefully, this will turn out to be a mini-outbreak, and it will be over soon."

Michael stepped up. "I'll go with you to the tenement."

"We have to stop by the hospital director's office first. Then we'll go back to Little Palermo. The director can contact city officials. Hopefully, we won't need the sheriff and public health to help us persuade this other man to let us check him out and if necessary, bring him here."

When they reached the doors of the Marine Hospital, the director met them, his face tense. "I'm glad you're back. I sent men out looking for you over an hour ago."

"But, sir, I've brought—" Phin began.

"There's no time for that now. Listen." The director

put his hand on Phin's shoulder. "There are three already, and I expect more. I've put Dr. Trasker in charge of the ward, but I want you to relieve him. Take Miss Morrison with you."

"But, sir—" Phin tried again.

"We're going to need supplies, and we're going to need to get the city health officials on board."

"Sir!" Phin grabbed the man's arm. "Yellow Fever. Aboard a ship called the *Mendoza*. They bypassed the quarantine, and they've got sickness aboard. I've brought a patient in with me, and there is at least one more, possibly two. Whatever is going on here will have to take a back seat to this."

The director paused. "Dr. Mackenzie, what do you think I'm talking about? There are three cases on the second floor now, and more will be coming in, I fear. The two suspicious deaths are confirmed as Yellow Fever. I've called in the city health already."

Natalie's throat constricted. It was worse than they feared.

"Three more? And I've brought in one just starting the toxic phase." Phin glanced at Natalie. "And there is another that should be checked out and possibly brought in."

The director took a deep breath. "I'm putting you in charge of the ward here. Follow the protocols we agreed on. Procure the supplies you need, and I will deal with the city health officials and formulate a plan of attack.

Write down the location of the other possible cases, and we'll track them down."

"Will you quarantine the entire crew of the *Mendoza*? And if so, where?" Michael asked.

The director looked at him as if just realizing he was there. "That will depend upon what the city and state health officials decide. Now, we have work to do. Dr. Mackenzie, Miss Morrison, the second floor west wing. Liase with Dr. Trasker." He nodded and left at a smart clip.

Phin started down the tiled hallway toward the staircase, and then paused, his hand on the wooden rail.

"What is it?" Natalie asked, almost bumping into him when he halted.

He inverted his lips, pressing them hard together as he rubbed his hand against the back of his neck as he looked from her to his brother. "This city isn't going to be a safe place, not with Yellow Fever. Not for either of you."

"Nor for you," Michael pointed out.

"I can't leave. I'll be needed here. But you two should go. I want you two to get out now before this turns into an epidemic."

"I can't leave people in need. And if this is an epidemic, there will be plenty of need." Michael crossed his arms and frowned. "I can help."

Natalie's spine straightened, her temper heating

that he would think she would run away either. "I'm not leaving either. As a nurse, I'll be needed. Anyway…"

Phin's gaze sharpened on her face, his dark eyes intent. "Anyway?"

She should come clean. Allay his fears in this respect. "Anyway, I'm now immune to Yellow Fever. I contracted the illness while in Panama. It's the reason I was invalided home early."

His hand dropped from the rail and took her arm. "You've had Yellow Fever? When were you going to tell me? I thought you looked as if you had been ill, but I never dreamed." He studied her face, and she knew he was looking at her eyes for traces of lingering jaundice.

"I am fine. The illness had run its course before I ever left Panama. The mission board thought I needed some time to recuperate and sent me home to do so. I can't believe you think I would leave."

Something flashed in his eyes, and his face hardened. "You've left before."

She flinched, and a sinking feeling hit her chest. "That was different, and you know it. Now, let's get upstairs and see these new patients." She marched ahead of him, rolling up her sleeves. "We have work to do."

❧

*P*hin dried his hands on the towel Natalie handed him, looking through the mosquito netting at the young man in the hospital bed, trying to keep the frustration out of his voice. He knew patient care at the hospital was important, but he felt trapped here. He should be in Little Palermo with Luca and the mobile unit. However, the director had insisted he remain in charge of this ward. Phin promised himself he would try again, as soon as the director returned.

"Keep an eye on the fever. If it goes up, and it probably will by evening, increase the dose of quinine as per the instructions in his chart."

Natalie nodded.

He didn't know what he would've done without her the past two weeks. She had practical experience in nursing fever patients, and she'd put that expertise to use, organizing the ward, creating schedules and supply lists, and training the handful of nurses assigned to the Yellow Fever ward.

Most were from the Marine hospital, but one had been sent by Michael. A black woman of considerable age who had nursed fever victims in Jacksonville, Florida, more than fifteen years before. A woman who, like Natalie, had survived the fever and was now immune. She had proven to be a stalwart.

Mary Sade—she was never called Mary, always Mary Sade—limped toward him, her arms full of clean sheets, favoring her left hip, which she said she'd hurt in a fall as a young woman. Phin suspected a poorly healed fracture was to blame, but he admired her grit in not letting that slow her down much.

"Doctah, that man in the last bed, he says he's feeling bettah, and he wants to leave. I told him to stay put until you said he could go, and if he didn't I would leg-rope him like a wanderin' hog, but you bettah go talk to him."

Phin smothered a smile at her homespun outlook, the first smile he had felt like raising for what seemed like a long time. Then he sobered. The pain and frenzy of the acute phases of Yellow Fever often required him to order restraints for his patients. He hoped that wouldn't be the case for Mr. O'Hara ever. "I'll speak with him." Weariness pulled at his limbs. Cases were beginning to surface more frequently, which made sense. Dr. Reed had proven that the incubation period in an *Aedes aegypti*, the mosquito that carried Yellow Fever, was about two weeks.

He started up the row of beds with Natalie at his elbow, where she'd been every time he needed her.

Natalie sighed and smoothed a stray strand of hair off her cheek, tucking it under her the kerchief she insisted upon wearing on the wards. She made a notation in a chart as they walked. Dark smudges hung under her eyes. No one had gotten much sleep lately. Their exchanges had been purely professional after his jab about her leaving had hit home on that first day they had worked together. Why had he said that when he'd promised himself he wouldn't bring it up ever again?

She closed the file folder and crossed her arms over it, hugging it to her chest. "It's always the same with fever victims, isn't it? The intial symptoms abate, and they are sure they are getting well. And most do, but the ones who don't....they have no idea what is coming."

The question that Phin had been wanting to ask her fell off his tongue before he could stop it. "Did you enter the acute phase?" He wanted to yank the question back, since he'd vowed not to ask about her time in Panama. She had shut that part of her life off from him, and he wanted it to stay that way. But it was too late. He'd asked.

She shook her head, and his muscles eased. "I never progressed that far, thankfully." Bleakness crossed her face. "We lost almost all who did."

"What was the mortality rate?" He kept his tone clinical.

"About one hundred cases that we know of were infected, and of those, twenty-six entered the toxic stage. Of those, nine died."

"Was it mostly foreigners affected?"

"A real mixture. Canal workers, government offi-cials, natives, and one missionary caught the sickness." She gave a rueful chuckle. "We'd best see about Mr. O'Hara before Mary Sade loses her patience."

Mr. O'Hara spotted them and began to sit up, but Phin motioned him back. "Not so quickly."

"But I'm feeling foin now. Woke up ready to take on the world." He gently thumped his narrow chest. "No fever, and the body's in good nick now."

Phin parted the mosquito netting and bent over the patient. "That's good, and I'm glad you're feeling better, but I'm going to have to insist you remain here with us for a few more days, just to make sure."

"A few days?" His red eyebrows went up. "What about me family? They fled north, and I need to go to them."

Phin thumbed up the man's eyelid. Still some lingering jaundice, but nowhere near as bad as it had been even twenty-four hours ago. He felt the man's forehead. Little or no fever. "How's your appetite?"

"I could eat a stove lid, I'm that peckish." He rubbed his belly. "That's a good sign, right?"

"A very good sign, but I'm going to have to ask you to trust me. We're under strict orders not to release any patient until he's been symptom free for at least six days. If you continue to improve"—Phin bent his best 'doctor look' on O'Hara—"and not give your nurses too much trouble, then you'll be free to go with our blessing in a week or so. Until then"—he turned to Natalie—"a bit of arrowroot gruel for Mr. O'Hara."

"Yes, Doctor." Natalie removed the clipboard chart from the foot of the bed and made a notation.

"Arrowroot?" O'Hara pressed back against the pillows, his freckles standing out like scattered gold dust. "Here I am wasting away, and you want to give me gruel? I need some meat. Beef and potatoes. Or failing that, some good old salted oatmeal."

Phin gave him a stern look, and Natalie shook her head, her lips in a straight line.

"Now, Mr. O'Hara." Natalie had parted the mosquito netting on the far side of the bed and now bent over the patient, straightening the covers and putting the man's hands and arms beneath the blanket. "You'll do exactly as the doctor says. Your system has been under attack the last few days, and it is going to take time to regain your strength. Take it from someone who knows. And stay under those blankets. You've had a raging fever, and we don't want you to get chilled." She gave him a quick smile.

O'Hara beamed up at her, and when she put her hand against his brow, he shot Phin a mischievous look. "If a pretty colleen like you were to sit beside me and hold my hand, I'd be sure to get better."

Phin found his neck stiffening, and a reprimand formed on the tip of his tongue. But before he could voice it, Natalie had removed her hand from the man's face and bent a stern look on him. "Mind your cheeky ways, Mr. O'Hara, or it will be Mary Sade attending you, and you're already nearing the end of your rope with her. She's liable to give you the rough side of her tongue."

Someone cleared his throat, and Phin turned. The director, suit rumpled and hair disheveled, stood at the foot of the bed, partially obscured by the netting. "Doctor, could I see you outside?"

"Nurse?" Phin inclined his head, and Natalie followed him out, adjusting the protection around the bed—protection not for the patient, but for the rest of the city.

The director leaned against the windowsill at the far end of the hallway, his shoulders stooped. "It's officially an epidemic now. The incubation period for the first cases is over, and more and more new cases are being reported. City officials are putting their plans into action, but we're behind this thing, and it's going to gain momentum before it slows."

"What is the action plan?" Phin asked.

"First, Dr. Kohnke, the director of the City Board of Health, has been in communication with national health officials, requesting help. President Roosevelt has been contacted, and he's promised aid. Second, we're going to implement the measures Dr. Reed took in Havana. Every cistern will be treated with kerosene and covered with a screen. Areas with standing water will be treated. Any new case of Yellow Fever will be reported, and a fumigation team will be onsite within the hour, spraying down the house and setting up a screened isolation room for the patient. Saturdays and Sundays, the citywide fumigation teams will be out spraying for mosquitoes. Acute cases will be brought to the hospitals." He ran his fingers through his hair and then dragged them down his face. He had aged what seemed a decade in the past two weeks.

"How are the other wards coping with the new cases?" Phin asked. Originally, his had been the only Yellow Fever ward at Marine Hospital, but as of this morning, there were now three.

"As well as can be expected. Fourteen new acute cases brought in today. We'll no longer be accepting cases until they reach the acute phase, otherwise we'll be overrun." The director held up his hands when Phin opened his mouth. "I know. But that's how it has to be. Local physicians are being allocated territories to oversee all over the city. We have to act as a team, and we have to trust our teammates. Your job is here in the hospital for now."

"My job is out there." He pointed over the director's shoulder through the window. "It's the whole reason we created the mobile doctor's office. I should be on the front lines, diagnosing new cases, educating the public, getting into Little Palermo and other immigrant enclaves where they need the most help." Phin jammed his hands into his pockets. He knew his work here in the hospital was important, but any physician could give nurses the basic orders for palliative fever care. He needed to be out in the city.

Natalie put her hand on his arm, but he shrugged it off. He didn't need placating or calming. He needed to do the work he had been called to do.

The director took his leave, and Phin sagged against

the windowsill. "I feel so hampered here. So closed in. I need to be out there, to see what's going on, to help all those people in need. I know there are dozens, maybe scores of people in Little Palermo who are falling ill, but they're either not reporting in or they're being overlooked."

"You can't do everything. Sometimes you have to trust others to do what you can't. You are needed here. You are making a difference. Are the people in your ward any less deserving of your help? Any less in need of medical care?" Natalie crossed her arms and tilted her head.

Her words brought him up short. She was right. He could do good here, and he would have to trust the local physicians, public health officers, and citizens.

God, help us. Help me. This is going to get worse before it gets better.

He pushed himself off the sill, squared his shoulders, and went back to the sick ward.

CHAPTER 5

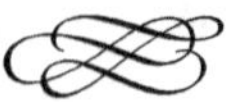

*N*atalie stripped the hospital bed, wadding the blood and sweat-soaked sheets in on themselves and stuffing them into the basket at her side. Her eyes smarted, both from sorrow and lack of sleep.

Mr. O'Hara had put up a valiant fight. But in the end, the fever had prevailed.

Mary Sade hitched by, stooping to pick up the basket. "Honey, you need to get you some rest. I put a glass of milk and a couple cookies on a tray in the first exam room. You get yourself in there and eat those up before one of the orderlies finds it."

Milk and cookies.

"I need to make up this bed. There will be a new patient in need of it soon."

"I kin do that. You run along. I tole the doctor to take him a few minutes too. You both been workin too hard. This ain't no sprint. We been at this a month, and we got aways to go yet."

A month since the first cases. A month of tense nursing, waiting for the second wave, and now seeing new patients daily. Every bed in the Marine Hospital was full, as were the beds in every other hospital in the city. The mayor had even opened the administration building of the Touro Infirmary, which had been slated for destruction this summer, as a charity ward, to house the sick. Marine Hospital was only admitting those in the toxic stage, so Natalie and Mary Sade and the rest of the nurses were hard-pressed.

Natalie slipped into the quiet exam room. As Mary Sade had promised, a tray sat on the desk. But it had two glasses of milk and four cookies on the plate. She sank into the chair and looked at the food, too tired to eat. Twelve hour shifts six days a week, and an eight hour shift on the seventh, for four weeks now.

A bead of sweat trickled down her temple, and she picked up a sheaf of papers from the desk to fan herself. The July sun beat against the drawn shade, trying to get in. The air was sultry, making even breathing an effort.

She leaned her head back against the chair and closed her eyes. Outside, yardmen clanged their tools and talked, one man giving orders. They were lighting the sulphur fires again to discourage mosquitoes. A rueful chuckle escaped her lips. They had become so commonplace, those stinking fires, that she hardly smelled them anymore. Her clothes reeked of sulphur, smoke, carbolic, and chlorine.

When the door knob creaked, she opened her eyes, though her lids were heavy. Phin put his hand on the frosted glass panel and opened the door wider.

She sat up straighter and found her hands checking her hair and kerchief, before she remonstrated herself for caring how she looked. She eyed him, taking in the rumpled white coat, the wrinkled trousers, the scuffed shoes. That, if nothing else would tell her of the hard hours he'd put in. Under normal circumstances, Phin took great pains with his dress, preferring to be well turned out at all times.

His dark hair hung over his forehead, and weariness clouded his normally bright eyes. "Did Mary Sade shoo you in here too?" he asked.

"Yes. I don't know where she gets the energy. She works just as long and hard as I do, but she still finds the vigor to boss me around."

"Not just you." He leaned against the examination table and reached for a cookie. "Aren't you having any?"

"I was trying to work up the energy."

His gaze sharpened, and he straightened, but she waved him back. "I'm fine. Just tired. I'm the one person you don't have to worry about getting the fever, remember? I've already had it."

He sagged back. "I remember, but humor me and eat a cookie and drink your milk."

She picked up the glass. "I will, but only because I

don't want Mary Sade to be disappointed." She took a sip, glad that the milk was still fairly cold. She couldn't abide warm milk. "What do you hear from the outside world?" With all her work, and with boarding on the top floor of this very building, Natalie hadn't ventured off the hospital grounds since the crisis began.

Phin finished his cookie and washed it down with his drink. "Nearly one hundred deaths have been reported, with more than a thousand cases of Yellow Fever. Who knows how many more unreported cases? Luca came by this morning for a moment. He's been working with Michael and city officials, trying to break down barriers in Little Palermo. That seems to be the part of the city hardest hit. They were heading out again today."

"Those poor people. So scared, so isolated by language and culture." She bit into a shortbread cookie, surprised at how good it tasted.

"Luca says the streets are bare. Shops are closed, the riverfront is a ghost town. According to the newspaper he brought with him, surrounding towns are enforcing a 'shotgun quarantine.' People trying to flee New Orleans are being met at train stations with shotgun-toting vigilantes who force them to stay aboard and move on or come back to the city."

"Can they do that?"

"They *are* doing it." Phin shrugged. "They're afraid. They don't want Yellow Fever in their town anymore than New Orleans wanted it."

Mary Sade knocked on the door. "Dr. Mackenzie, they's some folk here to see you." Her eyes swept the plate, and a motherly, chiding gleam entered her expression. "You eat all that up, you hear? I don't make special trays for folks only to have them not finish 'em up."

They reached for the last two cookies with a guilty start and then grinned sheepishly. "Where are these visitors? And who are these visitors?" Phin asked.

"The same fellow who came by for you this morning, and he has a big yella-haired man with him. I tolt them to wait out in the hall. They don't need to be traipsin' through the ward upsetting those poor souls in there." Mary Sade lurched away, her grizzled white hair poking out from its pins and her calico apron flapping.

"I used to think I was in charge of the ward." Phin pushed himself up and smoothed his hands down his coat front, frowning as if just realizing his rumpled state. "I look like I've been dragged through a knothole backwards."

"You look like you've spent hours bending over bedsides, treating patients." Natalie drained her glass and, in a total disregard of manners, wiped her lips with the hem of her apron. "Mary Sade was right. A little milk and cookies was just what I needed."

"Good. Natalie, you come too. You could use a few minutes more away from the ward." He offered his arm, and she rose and took it, conscious of him. They walked out into the hall, their footsteps echoing on the tiled floor.

Michael and Luca waited by the stairwell.

"Ah, *bella signorina*, so good-a to see you. You are a-working too hard. This terrible fever. It is too much." Luca advanced on her, taking her hands and squeezing them. He shook his big head, his beard brushing his chest. "So much-a sadness, yes? And always, we are-a finding you new people to look-a after, yes?"

Natalie squeezed back, though she wondered, with his huge hands, if he even felt the pressure. His dark eyes looked like burning coals, deep set and weary.

She turned to Michael. "How are you faring?"

He shrugged. "It's tough out there. Hardware stores are sold out of screening and mosquito netting. There isn't a mosquito bar to be had. Between the suphur fires and the fumigation, I don't know if I will ever breathe freely again." Putting his hands against his lower back, he stretched and winced. "I've spent so much time bending over fever victims' beds, praying for them, trying to bring some comfort, my back will never be the same."

"I can sympathize." Natalie nodded.

He turned to Phin. "Mother and Dad are very worried, as you can imagine. They've sent several telegrams to me. How about you?"

Phin nodded, patting his white coat pocket. "Three telegrams and a letter."

"You might want to think about answering them.

The message I got this morning is that they haven't heard from you in two weeks." Michael bent a knowing look on Phin. "They telephoned me this morning. I had to wait by the phone for an hour for the call to come through at the exchange. I assured them that you were fit the last time I saw you and that I would be coming out to the hospital today to check on you." He glanced at the crack of sunlight seeping around the window blind in the stairwell and stepped to one side, wincing at the bright light.

A low moan came from the ward, followed by a retching sound. Natalie turned to go assist the patient, but Mary Sade crossed the open doorway, basin in hand, comforting words already flowing from her lips. Natalie relaxed, sure that the sick man was in capable hands.

Michael grimaced. "Seen and heard too much of that lately." His hand went to his stomach. "I've never seen anything like it. I don't wonder that people fear Yellow Fever."

Phin put his hands into his pockets and leaned against the wall with a yawn. "Other than to come check on me, what brings you to the hospital?"

"Luca, actually. He found a patient for you, in a back alley down in Little Palermo. He's on his way up as soon as the orderlies can bring him. The nurses downstairs said he would need to be washed and clothed in hospital garb before they would let him on the ward."

"Standard admitting procedures. Can you tell me anything about him?"

"Si, dottore." Luca's shoulders stooped, and he shook his big head. "He is old-a man. Nobody to care for-a him. He come from-a Sicily only a few months ago, and he very scared. Scared of-a dottores and the polizia. He get sick, he-a hide. He no look for help."

Natalie and Phin shared a look. It was the same old story. She drew her handkerchief out of her apron pocket and dabbed her temples. What they needed was a good old-fashioned rainstorm to blow through and cool off the city and bring some relief to this oppressive heat.

She glanced at Michael, whose fair coloring was ruddy with the high temperature, but curiously, he wasn't sweating like the rest of them. He rolled his shoulders and winced again. A slight warning bell rang in the back of her head.

"Michael, do you have a headache?"

He was rubbing his temple absently, and when he looked at her, his pupils were dilated.

"Yes, but it's nothing. Not enough sleep, I daresay."

Her hand went out to touch his forehead, and her heart dropped as her fingers met his skin. "You're feverish."

Phin tensed, coming foreward to feel his brother's brow, to look into his eyes. "How long?"

"It's nothing, I tell you. A little headache. And I'm not feverish. It's hot outside." Michael brushed his brother's hand away. "You have plenty else to worry about."

"Come with me." Phin took Michael's arm. "Into the exam room. Luca, head down to the kitchen and tell them Dr. Mackenzie said they were to feed you. Ask for some ice cream. I know they've got some hidden away down there."

"Grazie, dottore, but what about Signore Michael?"

"We'll see to him. Come back up in half an hour or so."

Luca patted Michael on the shoulder. "You do what-a your brother says, yes?" His eyes were sober, though he tried to grin. "I will be back to see if you are being a good-a man."

Michael fussed. "Really, Phin. There's nothing wrong with me."

Natalie put her hand on Michael's other arm. "Please. It won't take long, and we'd rather be sure." The intensity on Phin's face, the fear in his eyes that she could tell he was trying to quell pulled at her. He loved his brother, a love forged in impossibly trying circumstances when they were both orphans so many years ago.

Michael sighed and tried another tack. "But what about the old man we brought in? Shouldn't you take care of him first?"

"Trust me, we'll put Mary Sade in charge of him, and he'll be as comfortable as we can make him in no time." She guided Michael toward the ward and the examination room just inside the door.

"Fine, but you'll see. I don't have the fever. I just have a bit of a headache. It will go away after I get some sleep." He protested all the way to the exam room where Natalie removed the glasses and tray from the counter and spread a clean sheet on the examination table.

"Sit up there." She pointed. "Remove your jacket."

Phin went to the sink on the wall and began to scrub his hands, his head bent.

Michael shrugged out of his suit coat. "You're awfully bossy, you know that?" The chiding irritation in his voice was new, and Natalie wondered if it meant he was in more pain than he was letting on. "And here Phin always said you were such a sweet, kind girl."

Natalie paused, her heart lurching. A sweet, kind girl. She drew a clean towel from the supply cupboard and handed it to Phin, not meeting his eyes. Did he still think that? Of course he didn't. He had been hurt and angry when she wouldn't marry him. Though they had worked together well this past month, he had kept everything on a professional level. No one would guess he had loved her enough once to propose.

When Phin concluded his examination, Natalie looked up from the notes she had been taking, summing up the symptoms the same way she knew Phin had. Fever, headache, backache, loss of appetite, fatigue. The early stages of the illness.

"That's it," Phin said, looping his stethoscope around his neck. "I've got a bed and a mosquito net with your name on it."

"But the hospital is only for acute cases." Michael stood and wavered a bit. Natalie reached out to steady him.

"The hospital is for people in need, and you need someone to care for you." Phin scrubbed his hands at the sink again. "I want you where I can keep an eye on you, and that means right here on my ward. Natalie, get him settled, and I'll check on the new patient Luca brought in."

Within the half hour, Natalie had Michael and their new patient, Aldo, in beds side-by-side in the ward.

Aldo, wizend, yellowed, and feeble, watched her with panicked, fever-bright eyes. When she tried to get him to drink some water, he refused, clamping his lips tight and shaking his head.

"But, sir, you must drink." His fever was soaring, and he was showing signs of dehydration.

"Here." Michael said. "Give it to me, and let him see me."

She parted the mosquito netting and gave him the glass. He took a long swallow, holding the water up so Aldo could see he had drunk about half. "He's afraid it's poisoned. He's afraid that since he's old and ill, you might try to get rid of him."

This time, the old man let her help him, and she cupped the back of his head, holding the glass to his lips. He drank a few sips and lay back, whispering, "Grazie."

Within a few seconds, he'd brought the water back up, accompanied by the dreaded "coffee grounds" emesis that indicated internal bleeding. Natalie helped him, holding the basin, wiping his mouth, mopping his face. He shivered, his body wracked with chills from the fever, and his eyes fluttered closed. He sank into unconsciousness.

Michael's eyes were wide, and he bit his bottom lip. Her heart went out to him, and she reached under the mosquito netting to hold his hand. "We're going to take the best care of you. And remember, most cases don't develop this far. Aldo here has several things working against him. He is elderly, and he went for far too long without any medical help or care. You are young and otherwise you've been in excellent shape, and you've gotten medical help right at the outset. We're going to support you through this, watch against dehydration or soaring fever, and keep you as comfortable as we can. You're going to be fine."

Michael squeezed her hand. "Thank you, Natalie. I apologize for insinuating earlier that you aren't a sweet, kind girl. Don't worry about me. God is still sovereign, and He is still good. Nothing will happen to me that He hasn't ordained."

She adjusted the netting over his bed, knowing he spoke the truth, but having to remind herself of it constantly.

"Oh, there's one thing. I didn't think to mention it during Phin's exam, because he's well aware of it already. I was born with a heart condition. I take digitalis every day. My pills…" He looked about uncertainly. "They were in my coat pocket."

A heart condition? Natalie swallowed and forced a smile. Fevers taxed the heart greatly. "We'll see that you get your medications. You need to rest now. I'll be back soon."

She gathered the tray and supplies she had used. When she reached the equipment closet, she found Phin, hands braced on the counter, head hanging.

Not knowing what to do but knowing she couldn't leave him, Natalie set the tray down gently and put her hand on his shoulder. "Phin?"

Without a word, he turned and put his arms around her, gathering her close and resting his chin on her head.

She said nothing, placing her arms loosely around his waist, offering him the comfort he seemed to need, trying hard not to savor the feel of being in his embrace.

"What will I do if God takes Michael away too?"

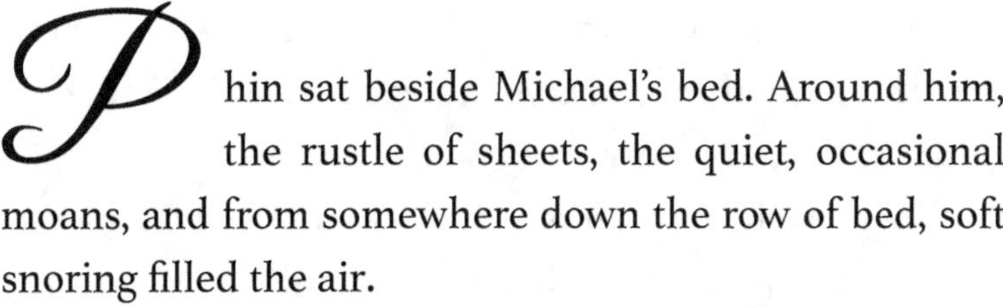

*P*hin sat beside Michael's bed. Around him, the rustle of sheets, the quiet, occasional moans, and from somewhere down the row of bed, soft snoring filled the air.

Mary Sade roamed from bed to bed, her lantern swinging gently in her hand. Two orderlies dozed on chairs, one at either end of the ward. The Regulator clock on the wall ticked softly.

Phin leaned forward, his elbows on his knees, fingers clasped. How many times had he tried to pray in the last hour, only to feel as if his mind and heart had hit a brick wall? Words wouldn't come.

On the surface, he had functioned, written orders, treated patients, met with the hospital director, and even showed a city councilman through the ward, outlining their methods and treatments. But underneath, he felt as if he walked on a rickety, swinging bridge over a vast abyss. If he looked down, the bridge would crumble and he would fall.

Michael had followed all the classic progressions of Yellow Fever over the past week. Soaring temperature, especially in the evening. Yellowing skin. No appetite. Joint pain. Headaches.

And then he had rallied, raring to get out of bed.

And through it all, Phin had held himself tight on the inside. Strict control, not looking inwardly at the thing that frightened him the most.

Michael stirred, moving his head from side to side on the pillow. After two good days where his symptoms had lessened, they had come roaring back this morning and worse than before.

To complicate matters, his heart was playing up. Phin had adjusted the digitalis so many times over the past week, he had created a chart of dosages and results and tacked it to the wall over Michael's bed.

And he'd telegraphed several colleagues around the country for advice. Dr. Charlie Mayo up in Rochester had been the most helpful, consulting his fellow clinic doctors and sending a detailed telegram in response as to possible treatment avenues.

Light flashed outside, quickly followed by a boom of thunder. Phin started, his head coming up. As if the lightning had torn a hole in the clouds, rain began to fall. The orderlies stirred and hurried around the ward closing windows as quietly as they could.

Mary Sade lumbered by, a pail in one hand, her lantern in the other. "Thank You, Jesus. Now maybe we kin get some relief from dis awful heat." Her dark skin glistened in the lamplight. "It's been hot enough to wilt a fencepost."

"Phin, are you still here?" Michael whispered, his lips tight. "You should be asleep."

He forced a slight smile. "So should you. How are you feeling?"

"Lousy." His voice rasped, and Phin parted the mosquito netting to offer him some ice chips. Phin had found that the ice, though it melted quickly in this heat, was better on his patients' stomachs than gulping water.

"Thanks. What time is it?"

"Nearly two in the morning. Let me listen to your heart." Phin reached for his stethoscope.

"How's Aldo?" Michael tried to peer through the netting to the next bed, but he let his head drop, screwing his eyes shut. "I feel as if a thousand bees are stinging the inside of my skull. Is that normal?"

Phin chuckled, trying to concentrate on Michael's heart rhythms but not wanting to miss an opportunity to tease his brother and hopefully cheer him a bit. "There's nothing normal about your skull. I've told you that before."

"Bully." Michael shot back.

"Brat." Phin grinned at their old banter.

Michael sobered. "Seriously though. I feel rotten. How's my ticker?"

"Surprisingly well, all things considered. The combination of medicines Dr. Mayo suggested seems to be helping. And all the cool baths to keep your fever down."

His brother squirmed and scowled, and if he wasn't so jaundiced, Phin suspected he would see Michael blushing. "I don't know which is worse, being given a sponge bath by Natalie or by Mary Sade. My dignity has suffered a severe blow."

Not having the heart to tell him that a sponge bath from a nurse would be the least of the indignities visited upon his brother in the coming days, Phin drew the sheet up. "You should rest."

"I don't want to rest. I want to talk."

"You need to conserve your strength."

"No, there are some things I need to say, just in case..."

"Stop that kind of talk. You're going to be fine. It won't be fun for the next few days, and it will take you a while to regain your strength, but you're going to come through this." Phin realized he'd fisted his hands on his thighs, and he made a conscious effort to relax. But his heart was pounding hard against his ribs, and a rivulet of sweat trickled down his spine. Thunder boomed again, rattling the windows, and he felt the concussion in his chest.

"Listen to me. I am no fool." Michael closed his eyes for a moment. "I have seen what this disease can do. I am ready to meet Jesus if that's called for. I'm not afraid. But I don't want to leave you without telling you..." A tremor went through him, and he took several deep breaths.

"Don't, Michael. You're taxing yourself."

His blue eyes, ringed with yellow from the jaundice and bloodshot from the attacking sickness, held Phin's.

"It's about Natalie." He swallowed. "I know you still love her. You always have. And she loves you."

"Stop." Phin put up his hand. He knew how he felt about Natalie. How he would always feel. But that's where it ended. She was amazing. Wonderful. Everything he wanted in a wife. But she didn't love him. Not enough to marry him.

And turning to her for comfort when he was scared had been a foolish thing to do, because it had caused to rear up all those feelings, so strong they nearly buckled his knees. Holding her in his arms, he had been spun right back to the moments before she had refused to marry him, those moments when everything had been possible and exciting and perfect...

She hadn't said a word about that embrace since. Her manner toward him hadn't changed. She was professional, helpful, and so dedicated to their patients that he had been forced to order her off the ward and to bed, or else she would still be here.

"I've watched her," Michael continued. "When she thinks no one is looking. She follows you with her eyes wherever you are. She is always finding ways to make your job easier, coaxing a smile out of you, encouraging you. When she watches you, she has such a wistful, almost aching look of longing on her face, as if she would like nothing more than to run right into your arms."

"You're being fanciful. It's the fever talking."

"No, it's not. Phin, I know you. Maybe better than anyone else in the whole world. I know the things that scare you, because we come from the same place. You're so scared of being alone, of those you love leaving you. Like your uncle did, dropping you in the orphanage and never looking back. Like Natalie did when she chose a missionary life over being your wife. You hold tight to the ones you love, but if you suspect they're going to leave you, you pretend you don't care. Like you did when you came to care for Mother and

Dad, but you were afraid they wouldn't love you, wouldn't adopt you and make us a family. You were terrible, breaking every rule you could, acting out, abandoning them before they had a chance to abandon you."

His words were barely a whisper now, and Phin knew what the effort to talk so much was costing him.

And he knew the truth of his brother's words. He did fear being abandoned by those he loved. And he tended to push away first so he wouldn't be hurt.

"Stop pushing Natalie away."

"Pushing her away? She's the one who left me, remember?"

"I know that, but since she's come back, have you talked to her? Really talked to her about what happened, why she made the choice she did, and whether she might have changed her mind about things now?" He moved under the sheet, as if everything hurt and he couldn't find a comfortable position.

Phin hadn't talked to Natalie. Not about anything personal.

And he didn't want to. Once you'd been hurt, why would you reopen the wound?

His physician's brain said, *To drain out infection. To clear out whatever might be festering in there.*

But his heart said, *That way is dangerous. If you peek under that bandage, it's going to hurt. And you don't want to be hurt like that ever again.*

"Rest, Michael."

"Did you send the telegram?" His eyelids fluttered closed.

"I did. They're praying. All of them."

A fleeting smile touched his lips.

Phin turned away, a hard lump in his throat. The next few days would determine Michael's future. The acute phase was just ramping up.

"God, how can You do this to me? I can't lose him." For the first time in a long time...since Natalie had turned down his proposal, Phin felt a niggle of doubt as to the goodness of God.

And a swelling of doubt that he could find a way to go on if God chose to take Michael home.

CHAPTER 6

$\mathcal{A}$ knock broke through Natalie's slumber, and she sat up, trying to focus. What time was it? Thunder rumbled, and she groaned. It had rained during the night—it was still raining—and she hadn't closed the window. The knock sounded again, and she reached for her robe, draped across the end of the bed. As she stood, she slipped in the puddle of rainwater on the linoleum floor. She skidded across the room and into the door, saving herself from a nasty fall by grabbing the doorknob and the edge of her dresser.

Thoroughly awake now, she wrenched the door open. "What?"

Avery Callan, secretary to Mr. Guillard, the mission board chairman stood in the hallway, his hand poised to knock again, water dripping from his raincoat and glistening on his face. At the sight of her in her night clothes and robe, he blinked and stared hard at the door jamb beside her.

"My...my...apologies for coming to your room like this. The porter downstairs didn't tell me this was your lodging, he just said you could be found in room 443. I can wait downstairs until you are...um...properly attired." Red suffused his cheeks.

She was covered from her throat to her ankles, but her hair lay in tumbled strands around her face and shoulders, escaped from the hasty braid she'd fashioned before falling into bed last night. And her feet were bare.

"What's happened? Why are you here?" *What time was it?* "I can't meet with you downstairs. I have to go on duty..." She glanced at the clock on the dresser. "...in about twenty minutes. We're working twelve-hour shifts until this crisis is over, and I am due to go on at the top of the hour." And she still needed to do a quick wash-up, dress, and bolt some breakfast. How had Michael fared last night? Had Phin gotten any sleep? Her mind raced with all she needed to do, even as her body told her she hadn't rested long enough.

Avery cleared his throat as he dug inside his rain-coat and drew out a damp envelope. "The director wished me to deliver this letter. There was a special meeting at the Mission last night and things have developed. Mr. Guillard asks you to come by the office at your earliest convenience."

"Why? What's happened?" She looked at the envelope, her name written in a neat, even hand on the front. "I can't leave the hospital. I'm needed here."

"Just read the letter. It will explain things. I have to go. It isn't seemly for me to be in a women's dormitory." Avery sketched a quick bow and hurried down the hallway, a trail of rainwater in his wake.

"Miss Morrison, I'm glad you're awake." Mrs. Bondurant, the hosptial matron called to her from the end of the dormitory hall. "Dr. Mackenzie needs you on the ward right now. Two more nurses have contracted the fever, and we're shorthanded."

"Yes, Matron. I'll be right there." Natalie closed her door, tossed the envelope onto her dresser, and threw a towel onto the floor, scrubbing with her feet to saok up most of the rainwater. Reaching the window, she closed it, peering out through the rain at the sodden hospital grounds. Two more nurses sick? She drew a clean uniform out of the wardrobe and laid it on the bed.

The mission director was going to have to wait. Once dressed, with her hair arranged neatly under her kerchief, she stuffed the director's letter into her pocket and headed to the ward.

When she arrived two floors down, every bed was full, and sometime in the night, three more cots had been squeezed in.

Rain continued to pound the windows on the south side of the building, but the orderlies were opening the windows on the north a few inches, because the air in the ward was stifling and thick with the scent of sickness.

Phin stood with Mary Sade at the far end of the ward, and when he looked up, he waved Natalie over.

"Say good night, Mary Sade." His voice was firm. "It's time for you to get some rest now."

"But my patients." The old woman swayed with fatigue, and both Phin and Natalie reached out to steady her.

"I've just had a good long sleep," Natalie said. "I'll see to the patients."

Mary Sade shook her grizzled head. "I ain't that tired."

"Doctor's orders." Phin motioned her down the ward, and she huffed and shuffled away.

Natalie went with her to the door. "I'll take good care of things. You don't have to worry."

"It ain't that." Mary Sade shook her head. "It's that I don't want to take the time. My house is clear over t'other side of the river. By the time I get there, I'll hardly have time to sleep before I got to get back."

"Ah, I see." Natalie tapped her lips, thinking. "I tell you what, why don't you just use my room here? It's right upstairs, so no time wasted."

"I can't sleep here." Her dark eyes widened. "What would the matron say? She don't much like me nohow."

"I'll square it with her. Dr. Mackenzie will order it if necessary. You know the matron will do anything for

Dr. Mackenzie." Mrs. Bondurant held physicians in high regard, their word was law, and she seemed to admire Phin especially.

Mary Sade finally agreed, after Natalie called Phin over and he ordered her upstairs. She grumbled, but she went.

"You should be asleep too. Did you stay here all night?" Natalie asked.

"Let's walk the ward." Phin's face was haggard as he evaded her question. "I'll catch you up on everyone's progress."

There was encouraging news for some who seemed to be recovering from the worst of the illness. Phin gave orders for these handful to be started on a light diet and encouraged to drink plenty of fluids.

"If I was certain they weren't still vulnerable to passing along the disease, some of them could be released to return home. But we haven't done enough studies to be sure when that time of contagion is past, so here they stay until every vestige of the jaundice has subsided and they are showing signs of regaining their strength."

Others had maintained throughout the night. Yellowed, sunken into the pillows, given pain medications to help, holding their own but not improving. The old man, Aldo, was in this group. He lay with his eyes closed, his skin parchment dry, his thin chest barely moving as he took slow breaths.

Then there were the ones who had worsened

overnight. Michael fell into this group. Jaundiced to an alarming degree, he groaned in his sleep, his lips in a grimace. His eyelids fluttered, and he arched his back. A trickle of blood leaked from his nose, and Natalie parted the netting to wipe his face.

Phin gripped the end of the bed, leaning over, his head falling. "He only wakens to vomit or from the pain. His skin is so yellow it's practically orange. His fever is dangerously high, and not even the sponge baths are working. I can't order an ice bath because the shock to his heart might kill him."

The anguish in his voice crushed Natalie's chest. She smoothed back Michael's blond hair, alarmed at the heat coming from his skin. The next twenty-four to thirty-six hours would be cruicial, if the disease took its normal course.

She stroked Michael's cheek once and emerged from the mosquito netting. "Phin—Dr. Mackenzie—" Mercy, she'd forgotten they were on the ward, where a nurse calling a doctor by his first name was forbidden. "You need to sleep. You've been awake for more than a day. You won't do Michael or any of your patients much good if you collapse. And if you contract the disease..." Her throat thickend at the thought of it. "You'll be more vulnerable to the worst of it if you're run down."

"I can't leave him." Phin shook his head. "I won't leave him. He's my brother."

Natalie heard both the conviction and exhaustion in his voice. He could be so stubborn at times. A woman hurried by with a pitcher of water and a towel over her arm. Her husband lay in a bed about halfway down the ward, and was one of the few who had family to help look after him. Natalie had thanked God for these family helpers many times over the last month as they lessened her load quite a bit.

"Then you should do what other family members do. Roll out a pallet beside his bed and go to sleep. I'll wake you if there's any change."

He raised his head and squinted, as if his eyes were too tired to focus without an effort. "Sleep on the ward?"

She crossed her arms. "I'd prefer it if you went home and slept in your own bed, but I can understand you not wanting to go. You and Mary Sade are two of a kind. It would be easier on the nurses and orderlies if you'd at least sleep on the couch in your office, but a pallet on the floor will work just as well. If anything comes up, I'll consult with Dr. Trasker on the ward across the hall, and when it's time, I'll wake you."

He was asleep within moments of hitting the pallet. Natalie worked her way down the ward, taking temperatures, recording heart rates, and seeing that all Phin's orders were carried out. In addition, she held buckets for those who were still in the vomiting stage, changed bed linens, and encouraged patients to try to drink.

All the while, she battled with how to reduce Michael's temperature without resorting to an ice bath.

The work was hard, heavy, and at times disheartening. Seeing so much suffering tore at her heart and brought back her own memories of fighting the illness herself. She tried to remember all the things that helped...her caregivers speaking in low voices, careful not to blunder into the bed or move her too quickly, squeezing a few drops from a washcloth onto her tongue when her stomach wouldn't tolerate her taking even sips of water.

The rain finally eased off, and she requested the orderlies to open the north windows wider. The south ones remained closed and shaded as the day heated up. Ceiling fans were turned on to move the air, which had cooled with the rain but now steamed as the humidity rose.

Mary Sade appeared in the doorway in the mid-afternoon.

"It's too soon. You should still be asleep."

"Child, when you get to be my age, it don't matter how tired you are, you don't sleep for too long before your old bones are telling you to get out of the bed." She spied Phin, still sleeping beside Michael's bed. "That po' man is 'bout out of his mind with worry. I never seen a man who cared so deep for those he loves." She patted Natalie's hand. "It's a blessed woman who is loved by a man like that."

She headed to the linen cart, and Natalie turned away. She had been loved like that once. And she had been blessed. But what could she have done? She was a missionary. She had been called. And Phin's life and calling were here.

In a few months, she would be back in Panama, and she would have to forget him all over again. But in the meantime, she decided she would treasure his friendship, cherish the time they could be together, and help and support him any way she could, both as a nurse and as a friend. All her life, she would have these months to cherish.

Thoughts of Panama reminded her of the Mission director's letter. Since she had a few moments, she drew it out, slipping into the hallway to read it.

Her eyes scanned the page, and her hands began to tremble. The mission board was satisfied that she was healthy enough to return to the field, and there was a ship departing from Mobile, Alabama, bound for Panama in one month's time.

A month? Just four weeks?

How could she leave New Orleans in the middle of the crisis? Yellow Fever epidemics lasted until for months...until colder weather drove away the mosquitoes.

And yet, she'd begged the mission board to get her back to the field as quickly as possible.

But what about her patients here?

What about Michael Mackenzie? How could she leave not knowing if he would survive?

And what about...Phin? There was so much that had

been left unsaid between them. When she had refused his marriage proposal, he had left her there in the park where he had asked her to be his wife, and she hadn't spoken to him since. The letter she had written him aboard the ship to Panama had never been mailed. She refused to leave again without speaking to him, but how could she bring up anything from their past when the present was so urgent and unsettled?

She slowly folded the director's letter and returned it to her pocket. He requested her presence at the office as soon as possible to discuss the details.

Her heart and mind were torn.

Her father's words, spoken in a rasp from his deathbed, rang in her ears. "You will have to go for me, Natalie. You'll have to be the missionary I never got to be. Your place is in Panama."

But something else in her heart whispered, *Your place is here.*

Which one was she to believe?

~

*P*hin woke slowly, his brain hazy, his shoulder and hip sore from sleeping on the floor. He kept his eyes closed, listening. The rain had stopped. A bedframe creaked. Metal touched glass. Sheets rustled.

He forced his eyelids to part. From his vantage point, he could see all the way to the far wall under all the cots. He would have to commend the janitorial staff. Not a trace of dust to be seen. Disjointed thoughts from his cotton-wool brain.

Forcing himself to sit up, he grimaced. He'd slept in worse conditions than this through most of his youth, but he wasn't a kid anymore. He creaked worse than an old barn door. He scrubbed his hands down his face, feeling the stubble rasping against his palms.

Remembering why he'd slept on the floor, he scrambled up and ducked under the mosquito netting of Michael's bed.

Mary Sade sat on the far side of the bed, sponging Michael's face and neck, her lips moving in what Phin knew were prayers for his brother.

"How is he?" The color of Michael's skin alarmed him but not as much as the tight, gasping breaths and the grimace contorting his brother's face. Touching his skin, Phin winced. He was burning up. The fever must be putting his heart under tremendous strain.

"Oh, he fightin' hard. I never seen a man fight so hard. Doctah Trasker thinks it won't be long now until we know, one way or t'other." Her gnarled hands wrung out another cloth.

"Mary Sade, I have the socks. Should we give it a try?" Natalie appeared at the foot of the bed, and paused. "Oh, you're awake."

"How long has he been like this? Why didn't you wake me?" Anger fueled by fear ripped through him.

"Don't yell." Brian Trasker hurried up. "I told them

to let you sleep. I've been here covering for you. You've slept most of the day."

"Shall we go ahead, Dr. Trasker?" Natalie asked.

"Yes. It can't do him any harm, and it might help."

"What are you doing?" Phin asked. "And why wasn't I consulted on a change in Michael's care? He's my brother." He spoke loudly, and Aldo, in the next bed groaned, throwing his arm up to cover his eyes.

Brian took Phin's elbow and steered him away from the bed. "We will consult in private so we don't disturb the ward."

When they reached the privacy of the exam room, Phin crossed his arms, his eyes gritty, irritated at being pulled away from Michael's bedside. "Well?"

"Phin, relax. We're all running on high stress and little sleep." Brian pinched the bridge of his nose. "Michael's holding his own. We're doing what we can to reduce the fever."

"What was Na—Miss Morrison doing with those socks?" Phin demanded.

"It's Mary Sade's idea. Something she says she's tried before. Since we can't use ice on Michael because of his heart, and sponging him is only getting us so far."

"Putting sock on him isn't going to cool him off."

"Listen. The procedure is to put warm cloths on his feet to increase the blood flow, then put socks soaked in ice water on him to cool that blood quickly, repeating often. I have no idea if it will work, and we'll continue with the sponge baths and medications, but I figure it can't hurt. Look, it might be an old wives' remedy, but some of those are born out of some truth." Brian tilted his head, giving Phin a long, compassionate look. "It's hard when it's family. For now, why don't you let me be his doctor and you be his brother?"

Phin forced himself to calm down. It wasn't easy. Seeing Michael in such distress sent panic waves crashing through him. *Please, God, don't let him die.* He closed his eyes, taking a deep breath.

"All right. I'm sorry. It's just..."

"I know." Brian punched his arm. "You care. That's natural. But we care too. And not just about Michael. About you too."

They returned to the ward.

"Mary Sade," Brian said. "Phin's going to sit with Michael and take over for you."

Phin pulled a chair up to Michael's bedside. Mary Sade handed over the wet cloth with a smile. "You be letting me know when you need more water or anything else, you hear? I'm gonna help Miss Natalie."

He nodded and bathed Michael's hot face.

Natalie lifted Michael's legs, and Mary Sade put an oilcloth underneath them. Applying the warm cloths, they worked together until Michael's yellowed legs turned a dull red.

"Now, get them cold wet socks on him." Mary Sade took one from the bowl of ice water, and without bothering to wring it out, slipped it on one of Michael's feet.

He grunted, his brow furrowing, and he sucked in a deep breath.

Phin patted his shoulder while Natalie was quick with the other stocking. Mary Sade then picked up a hand fan and swished it over Michael's legs and feet.

Aldo groaned from the next bed, and Natalie went to his side, helping him sit up enough to drink a few sips of water. Phin studied her as she cared for the little Italian. She'd lost some weight over the past month, and she hadn't been too robust even then, though now he knew why. But she hadn't murmured a word of complaint over the long hours, the heartbreaking work, or the changes in her plans.

She had been everything he remembered about her and more. And his heart longed for her more intensely than it ever had.

Five years ago, he had vowed to put her out of his mind and heart. He had refused to even say her name aloud. He had gone on with his life, deliberately not thinking of her, throwing himself into work and his family and ignoring the giant hole in his heart.

And all for naught. Because his love hadn't diminished. He hadn't been able to eradicate his feelings for her.

Now, God had brought her back into his life when he needed her most. Needed her nursing skills, yes, but needed her presence, her hopeful outlook, her rock-steady faith.

But not just those things. He had need of her as a

man needs the woman he loves. For comfort and solace, for life and love and a future built with each other.

Bathing Michael's face, he questioned his courage. Michael said she still loved him. Did he dare believe it was true? Did he dare to offer her his heart one more time and hope that she would accept it, accept him?

Did he have the right to, if her calling truly lay in a foreign land?

What was right?

What was going to cause either of them the least hurt?

Could he live with the pain if she turned him down again?

Could he live with the regret if he never asked?

Hours later, Phin half-dozed in his chair. Darkness had fallen again, the ward was quiet. Mary Sade's shoes swished on the floor, and Natalie's voice drifted through his mind as she spoke to a patient down the way.

Michael stirred, and Phin jolted awake.

"Some doctor you are, sleeping on the job." Michael's voice was raspy and dry, but having him lucid and talking sounded like sweet music to Phin.

"You're awake." Phin parted the gauzy curtain and touched his skin. It was cool and dry, with a bit of elasticity and a sheen of sweat. Bending quickly, he put his ear to Michael's chest. His heart beat, slow and regular. Phin straightened, his lips parting in a smile.

"I knew you'd make a good doctor. You can tell

awake from asleep." Michael cleared his throat. "Can I have some water?"

As Phin turned, Natalie pulled aside the mosquito netting across the bed. She held a glass. Phin helped Michael raise up enough to drink. "How are you feeling?" he asked, when Michael's head lay on the pillow once more.

"Like I fell down a mine shaft?"

"I can understand that. You've been very sick."

Natalie wiped Michael's face and dried it with a clean towel. "Do you have any pain? Are you hungry?"

He grimaced. "Some, but not as much as before. And yes, I am. But mostly I'm thirsty."

Mary Sade spoke from the end of the bed. "I sure am glad to see you doin' better, Preacher. These two been 'bout beside themselves with worry over you. God been answering their prayers all right."

Brian plucked the chart from the hook at the foot of the bed and drew a pencil out of the breast pocket of his white coat. "I'm prescribing some broth and crackers for you, Michael, as well as some tea. If that stays put, we'll think about some more adventurous foods later."

Phin looked at Natalie, and she smiled at him, a full-force, full-of-joy smile that he hadn't seen on her face in more than five years. It hit him like a punch to the heart. How could he let her go out of his life again? If the chance to tell her how he felt ever came, would he be brave enough to take it?

atalie gave instructions to the nurses coming on shift for the night before scooting a chair beneath the mosquito netting tent surrounding Michael's bed and sinking down onto it. She was so tired, but it was a good kind of tired, knowing she had done good work, and that today, on the men's Yellow Fever ward, they had lost no patients and there had been several, like Michael, who had made marked improvements.

"You're looking better all the time." She checked his pulse. "You're going to be yellow and tired for quite a while, but I'd say you're definitely on the mend."

"I gather the outcome was in doubt there for a while?"

"You were very sick." Releasing his wrist, she clasped her hands in her lap. "Phin was very worried. We all were."

"Where is Phin?"

"At a meeting of hospital, city, and federal health officials to assess how effective the efforts at mosquito control are. He'll be back later, though I hope he at least takes the time to eat and get some sleep."

"You should too."

"That is my next move. As soon as I drum up the energy."

"Before you go, can we talk?"

She sat up straighter. "Are you hurting?"

"No, no, not like that, though I will admit...I am hurting, for you and Phin."

"For us? Why?"

"Because I'm not blind. You're in love, and you're miserable." His eyes sought hers, full of compassion. "Tell me what's going on. Maybe I can help. At the very least, I'm a good listener."

Her lips trembled at his kindness and the weight on her heart. "I am in love. I have been since just about the first time I met Phin. But I shouldn't be. I have to return to Panama."

"But why?"

"It's my calling. I promised my father on his deathbed that I would fulfill the call to be a missionary. His dream was to take the gospel to the people of Panama, but because of his ill health, he never got the chance. So I need to go in his stead. He said that when I was born, he dedicated my life to the Lord and the people of Panama, knowing he would never be able to go himself. He had contracted diptheria, the same illness that took my mother right after my birth. He was partially paralyzed and never walked again."

"And he commissioned you as an infant to go in his place?"

She nodded. "Not just as an infant. We spoke of it many times. It was just always understood. I didn't mind. Not at all. I wanted to go. Until I met Phin. Like I said, I fell in love with him before I knew it, and then he proposed, and it caught me off guard."

"Natalie, have you ever considered that you were carrying a burden that wasn't yours? Perhaps it wasn't right of your father to ask you to fulfill his dreams. If God had truly called your father to be a missionary in Panama, He would have made a way for him to get there."

"But," Natalie protested, "I know God called me to be a missionary. He said to go to the 'uttermost parts of the earth'."

"He also said to go to Jerusalem, Judea, and Samaria. He was telling the disciples that they were to spread the gospel wherever they were. We're all missionaries, and you don't have to cross an ocean to qualify. You've been around New Orleans. A mission field opens up around every corner. Sicilians, Irish, English, German, good old-fashioned Americans. While I admire your passion for the people of Panama, it would be wrong to think those were the only people you were called to serve. What I do know is that any decision you make about Phin shouldn't be motivated by an unfair burden placed on you by either your father's last wishes or taking one phrase of one verse out of context." His voice was kind, brotherly. "I'm not saying you shouldn't be a missionary to Panama. Perhaps you should. But only after careful considera-tion and understanding what Jesus truly meant in the Great Commission."

Natalie considered his words. On the one hand, she knew he was correct, that Christians were to spread the gospel wherever they were...but on the other, she had always thought that being a missionary meant leaving your country to head to a foreign land. Could she fulfill both the Great Commission and honor her father's wishes if she stayed in America? Or was she merely trying to justify staying so she could be with Phin?

Not that Phin had asked her to stay. Not this time.

If he did, what would she say?

CHAPTER 7

*P*hin headed up the hospital steps, bouyed by the council meeting news. Their efforts were working. Fewer than two hundred deaths so far. And while that was still a shocking number, if their estimates held, they were on track for fewer than five hundred. Almost a tenth of the number who had died in the last major Yellow Fever outbreak in New Orleans.

And Michael was on the road to recovery. Phin had called his parents in St. Louis before his meeting.

"Praise the Lord!"

His mother had broken down, crying, when he told her the news, dropping the phone. His father, Sam, had picked up the receiver.

"I take it you have good news, son?"

"I do. He's turned the corner. His fever has broken, and the pain is subsiding. It's early days yet, but he's going to make it."

Phin heard his father swallow hard and suck in a deep breath. "That's the best news possible. And what about you?"

"I'm fine. Better now that Tick's on the mend. I can't tie up this line long, but I wanted to let you know the good news."

"Wait, son, before you go. Your mother and I will be coming to New Orleans."

"You can't. The danger isn't over."

"Nevertheless, we've been praying about it, and we feel we should come. Michael will need some care, and your mother is concerned about the children. There are bound to be many orphans as a result of the fevers, and she's determined...and I am too...that we should be there to care for as many as possible."

Phin leaned against the wall, closing his eyes and holding the receiver to his ear. It was just like his parents to think of orphaned children at a time like this.

"I understand. But please, at least wait until fall. There's a travel ban in place anyway, that you can't break, but I will let you know the minute it lifts. Give my love to Mother and the grands, and everyone there. Michael will write or call as soon as he can."

His parents, starting an orphanage in New Orleans. Having them here would be wonderful. Michael with his ministry to sailors and stevedores, his parents ministering to the city's orphans, and himself, with his mobile doctor's office, ministering to those who called New Orleans's poorest neighborhoods home.

Bounding up the stairs, he went first to the Women's Yellow Fever Ward across the hall from his own. "Brian, can you cover for me for a half hour or so? I'm on duty now, but there's something I need to do."

"Sure. Anything wrong?" Brian looked up from his notes.

"Nothing to worry about. And thanks." Phin headed for his own ward.

Michael was propped up, half-sitting, and Mary Sade was helping him eat some broth. Phin stopped at the foot of the bed. "Have you seen Miss Morrison?"

"She went to the pharmacy. She be back soon." Mary Sade eyed him. "You need her?"

In so many ways.

His expectation must've shown on his face, because Michael mirrored Mary Sade's expression. "Should I say a prayer or two?"

"That would be appreciated."

Mary Sade sniffed. "'Bout time."

Natalie appeared in the ward doorway, a packet in her hand. She gave it to one of the orderlies, and Phin started her way, taking her hand and leading her out of the ward.

"What is it?" She asked, trotting alongside to keep up.

"We're going for a walk."

"A walk? It's almost dark."

"You used to like walking with me in the dark." He laced his fingers with hers, glancing down at her. She wore a look of confusion and fluster. Good, she'd confused and flustered him plenty.

Once outside, he took the gravel path leading around the hospital to the parklike grounds in the rear. In the courtyard, parked for the night, his mobile doctor's office stood in a row of ambulances. The wagon had been pressed into service over the past few weeks and had lost some of its luster, but he didn't mind. Hopefully, it would see many more years of service as he treated his patients in New Orleans.

When they reached the little flower garden at the center of the park, Phin stopped. The sun had slipped beneath the horizon, but its soft afterglow lit Natalie's face.

He took both her hands in his. His mouth was dry, and his pulse hammering. "Now that I've got you here, I don't know how to start."

Her eyes caught the fading sunlight, wide and amber. "Phin, please, may I go first?"

A shaft of pain hit him. "No, not if you're going to tell me you're going back to Panama. I need to have my say first. Natalie—do you know, I haven't said your name aloud in five years?—Natalie Mae Morrison, I love you. I loved you five years ago, I loved you the entire time you were away, and I love you now, more than ever. I cannot bear to have you go out of my life without telling you how I feel. I know with certainty that my work is here in New Orleans, and I want to share that work with you. I want to share my life with you. I know you may say no, but there it is. I love you. I want you to stay. I want you to be my wife."

Now that the words were out there, he held his breath, half-wishing he hadn't spoken. If she refused him, if her convictions remained the same, how would he go on?

The wait, while only a couple of seconds, stretched out interminably.

Then her hands came up, cupping his cheeks. "Phin," she blinked hard. "Phin, I am so sorry I hurt you. I love you so much. I don't ever want to hurt you again."

His hands came up to cover hers. What did this mean?

"Did you know your brotheris a very wise man? He showed me the error of some of my thinking." She shook her head. "It's too much to go into now, but suffice it to say, I don't regret my time in Panama, but that time has passed. My place is here now. With you." She pressed her trembling lips together for a moment, and his eyes zeroed in on the movement. "I love you, Phin Mackenzie."

She had barely gotten the words out before he had crushed her to his chest in a tight embrace. He kissed her, fiercely, with all the longing of five interminable years, with all the hope of the years to come.

When he was almost dizzy with the need to breathe, he tucked her head under his chin, kept her wrapped in his arms, and closed his eyes.

"Are you absolutely sure?" He had to know. They were in the midst of trying times, emotional times, and he didn't want her to have regrets.

Her arms tightened around his waist, her hands pressing into his back. "I am sure. I've thought and prayed and considered, and all the time, the only peace I could find was when I thought of staying here with you."

Phin didn't know how long they stood that way, holding one another, but he savored every minute.

The clatter of hooves drew his attention. One of the hospital ambulances turned into the courtyard. Another case.

Natalie stirred. "We should go."

Phin couldn't resist one more kiss. "To tide me over." He laced his fingers with hers for a moment. "I love you, Natalie."

"I love you too, Phin. Let's get to work in our mission field."

Did you enjoy this book? We hope so!
**Would you take a quick minute to leave a review
where you purchased the book?**
It doesn't have to be long. Just a sentence or two telling
what you liked about the story!

Receive a FREE ebook and get updates when new Wild
Heart books release: https://wildheartbooks.org/
newsletter

ABOUT THE AUTHOR

Best-selling, award-winning author **Erica Vetsch** loves Jesus, history, romance, and sports. When she's not writing fiction, she's planning her next trip to a history museum. You can connect with her at her website, www.ericavetsch.com and you can find her on Facebook at **The Inspirational Regency Readers Group** where she spends way too much time!

If you love historical romance, check out the other Wild Heart books!

The Songbird and the Surveyor by Denise Farnsworth

A marriage of protection. A past full of pain. In Georgia's wild gold country, love might strike when it's least expected.

Genevieve Gillbard knows she's no longer safe in the rough-and-tumble gold rush town when she overhears her controlling guardian's plot to steal gold from a local mine owner. It takes every ounce of her courage to escape, and now she'll do anything to keep herself safe, even accept a temporary marriage of convenience from a man who clearly wants nothing more than his independence.

After losing his first wife, surveyor Jesse Holden swore never to let anyone close enough to need him again. But when he discovers the woman he knows as the Songbird of Auraria injured and unconscious in the woods, he can't abandon her, not with the memory of his failure to protect his wife hanging over him. He'll keep this woman safe until she's out of harm's way, even if it means doing the one thing he swore he'd never do again.

As Genny recovers under Jesse's care, she discovers he's nothing like the manipulative men of her past. But can she trust him with her heart—knowing he plans to leave as soon as her guardian is brought to justice? And even then, she fears the sham marriage might not be enough to keep her safe from her guardian's long reach.

Petticoat Ranch by Mary Connealy

Sophie Edwards has survived two years in the Texas wilderness with four daughters and her wits. When a stranger falls injured near her hidden cabin during a thunderstorm, she discovers he's the spitting image of her late husband—because Clay McClellen is her husband's twin brother, a man who never knew his brother existed.

Clay came to Texas seeking justice for his brother's murder. What he finds instead is a ready-made family, a rundown ranch, and a fiercely independent woman who doesn't need rescuing—even when danger comes calling. Sophie may have pulled him from a flooded creek, but Clay is determined to be the protector she deserves, whether she wants one or not.

As vigilantes close in and old enemies resurface, Clay and Sophie must learn to trust each other and God's plan. But can a mountain man used to solitude embrace life with four talkative daughters? And can Sophie open her guarded heart to love again—especially when the man looks exactly like the husband who broke it?

A heartwarming tale of second chances, faith, and finding love in the untamed West.

~

The Reverend's Second Chance by Lauralyn Keller
A buried secret in Harmony Springs could cost a

pastor and a teacher their careers—and their second chance at love.

Lydia Jefferson buried her dreams long before the death of her husband. Now she's locked her heart to men for good. In Harmony Springs, she's finally found freedom from the shameful failure and loss of her past —until her childhood sweetheart arrives to be the new pastor.

Samuel Allen never thought he'd love again, not after his fiancée walked out of his life. But when his first church assignment sends him to Harmony Springs, he finds himself face to face with the woman who disappeared from his life seven years before. Could this be a second chance at love? Unfortunately, she wants nothing to do with him.

When an orphaned child brings Lydia and Samuel together again, can they face the pain of their past and learn to trust each other enough to build a home?